Jungle

Stories from *The Sewanee Review*

Gladys Swan

Jungle

Stories from *The Sewanee Review*

Gladys Swan

SERVING HOUSE BOOKS

Jungle: Stories from *The Sewanee Review*

ISBN: 978-0-9977797-2-1

Cover art: "Jungle," painted by Gladys Swan, photographed by Monte Nevins

Serving House Books logo by Barry Lereng Wilmont

Published by Serving House Books
Copenhagen, Denmark and Florham Park, NJ
www.servinghousebooks.com

Member of The Independent Book Publishers Association

Friends of Poets & Writers

First Serving House Books Edition 2017

"Jungle" received the Andrew Lytle Fiction Prize as the best story published in *The Sewanee Review* in 2015.

For George Core, who first published these stories—
with appreciation for his support and encouragement
over the years.

Contents

"A Literalist of the Imagination"

There is a moment, in the second of this collection's ten stories, "The House on the Lake," in which the protagonist thinks it was "as though what could be imagined could, with enough passion, take form." Gladys Swan might have been writing about her own imaginative fiction, in which with highly crafted language, she creates illusions which are another way of knowing, becomes—what Yeats suggested—"a literalist of the imagination" and presents "imaginary gardens with real toads in them."

In another story, midway through the book, a magician in a broken-down carnival seemed to Alta, whose stream of experience is the narrative voice, "to want to climb to ever higher steps of illusion." Gladys Swan is the source of illusion, whose mirages become almost palpable and make the reader know, in recapitulating these stories, a kind of a truth in the mirage.

Broken-down carnivals, peopled by tigers, elephants, arthritic camels, magicians, a pair of grounded aerialists, a band of carny gypsies moving across a Rabelaisian moonscape that approximates the American Southwestern desert lend fertile ground for Ms. Swan's imagination. In two of these stories ("Jungle" and "Carnival for the Gods"), carnivals provide the settings in both real and metaphorical terms. In fact the latter, which was published as a short story, grew over the years, as Ms. Swan's fascination at imaginary carnivals (with "real" tigers in them) increased, into a quintet of novels about the carnival people with dreams that come down to earth: Alta, the "Dream Girl" and Dusty "Gold Dust," the aerialist and her catcher; Amazing Grace, the snake lady; "a giant and a midget who fought and were inseparable"; an animal trainer "who was convinced a woman lived inside his tiger, the only woman he'd ever wanted...." A short story with characters sufficient in number and substance to play the cast of five novels – Gladys Swan had a full-fledged vision.

However, the ten stories in this collection are a full vision as well, each on its own and the collective ten, a vision of how one woman sees the world through her passionate imagination, and that imagination takes form.

Ms. Swan's language, too, is alive and refined, tempered by the frequent warm nudge of humor; in speculating on the animal trainer's conviction, Alta "wonders if anybody had ever tried fucking a tiger?" (Which line Ms. Swan reads aloud at public readings in an off-hand, speculative voice similar to Mae West's.)

Alta loves "bright colors: reds that could have come from the throat of a trumpet," and there are splashes in the titles Ms. Swan selects for the stories—"Jungle," "The Orange Bird," "A Garden Amid Fires," "The Ink Feather".... After all, she is an artist who works in oil, watercolor, and gouache (she painted the cover for this book – as she's done for other books for twenty years or more) as well as in poems, essays, novels, and stories. She is a multi-artist, and the one art informs the other.

From 1981 to 2015, all ten of these stories have been published in *The Sewanee Review*—one of the U.S.A.'s prime literary journals, published quarterly since 1892. The title story won the Andrew Lytle Fiction Prize for the best story published in the journal in 2015. Many Nobel Laureates, Pulitzer Prize winners, and other illustrious authors have seen print there. Though art is not a competitive sport, the competition is fierce.

These stories are a prestidigitation in which the cloak of verisimilitude is nicely laid out for us and becomes real, becomes true. It is a kind of magic, that magic available to man: not the submission to, but the revolt against "this due degree of heaven-bestowed blindness" – the revolt that changes reality, via creations of the imagination, which can complete for us the insufficiencies of human existence.

Thomas E. Kennedy
Copenhagen, February 2017

Thomas E. Kennedy's more than forty books include novels, story and essay collections, and literary criticism, most recently the four novels of *The Copenhagen Quartet*, 2010-14 (www.CopenhagenQuartet.com).

JUNGLE

When I was a kid I hardly had a name. It felt like I was kin to animals. Maybe that was on account of something you couldn't give a name to—a wildness that lived in us both. There wasn't a whole lot then to tie me to the human world. I couldn't remember anyone's calling me by a syllable that drew me to the sound, made me want to take it on. Oh, I might hear "Hey you," or "Get on over here, you little stinkweed." This from the one who stood in for a father, if he stood anywhere at all. Not that I ever called him *Daddy*. A mouth—that's what he was—all scrunched up like he'd bit off too much of life and wanted to spit out the taste before he choked on it.

His name was Priam Gillespie. He hated that name, the way people pronounced it *Pry-am* or *Pree-am*. Every once in a while somebody would say, "What the hell kind of name of that?"

"It's what comes of having a librarian for a mother," he'd explain. "Damn her hide anyway."

Every once in a while, maybe in a store or the bank, somebody would call him *Mr. Gillespie*, and I'd look around for the stranger I thought they were speaking to. Sometimes he called me *Miss* or *Missy*. "Don't give me any of that guff, Missy." Or *Toots* when I was coming on to being a woman. "Oh, so now you're getting ready to strut your stuff, eh, Toots?" I wanted to kick him.

Somewhere there was a birth certificate with my paper name. But it just fell by the wayside—it had nothing to do with me. Whenever somebody spoke it, I didn't look around or say a word. "What's your name, honey?" some folks would ask, and when they saw a blank, they'd smile down into my face, as if getting closer would turn on the light bulb, and ask, "What's your dolly's name?"

It wasn't a real doll, just a sock with stuffing in it, and button eyes and a mouth sewed on. "*Name*," I'd tell them.

"*Name*—that's her name?" That would tickle them all right. And Priam would say, "She's just ornery—always has been." Maybe *Ornery* should have been my name.

"Just wait till I can send you over to Texas," he'd say every once in a while, like he was trying to get even with me, "and let that mama of yours do what she was created for." And then, under his breath, "If she'd quit running around long enough to do anything useful."

A voice from long ago ran like a tune through my head. I could remember someone holding my hand: I could almost feel the way it curled around mine—warm and a little moist—even when I couldn't attach a person to it. Was that my mama? I couldn't see her—I was never sure. I really couldn't remember any mama at all. Seems like I'd just happened in this place, like a scrap of paper blown in by the wind.

Every once in a while I'd ask when I was going to Texas, but Priam would pull a face and say, "Mind your business. I got troubles enough as it is."

It took me a while to get a name, as I'll tell you, and it happened in a way I never expected. That seems the way of things—full of surprises. My life started changing when I was about eleven—when Priam got hold of a piece of land across the highway. Took it for collateral from a Mexican family who'd got into his clutches. I used to play horse with their kids, and Carolina and I liked to braid each other's hair. Hers was long and black and glossy, and I loved to get my fingers in it. Sometimes I'd eat dinner in their adobe hut—tortillas with beans, and enchiladas with red chili sauce, and sopapillas with honey. I can almost taste the food yet— the chili hot in my mouth, then the sweet taste of the sopapillas— and the way Carolina's mama filled my plate and teased me and treated me like one of her own kids. The day they all left, I stood there like a stone, watching them pack up their truck with boxes and baskets, lifting up the couch, then the kids piling in, lining up on it, their dog in the middle, a friendly brown mutt with a long body and little short legs named Chico, who was always part of our games. Then they were gone in a cloud of dust.

Vaya, conmigo. Vaya, amiga. Muy lejos de aquí. Let me grab my stick and trot my pony—*ta da, ta da, ta da.*

Their adobe hut sat empty for I don't know how long—the wind shuffling a few tumbleweeds and scraps of paper in its direction. A little way off were some dilapidated sheds and corrals that had once kept horses or cattle, plus an abandoned shack that people said was haunted by the ghost of Geronimo. I never figured out what he'd be doing in the neighborhood unless he was really down on his luck. But us kids had played like he was still inside and whoever saw him gave out a yell and took off. I never saw him, but I pretended I did and yelled and ran with the rest.

Just opposite was our place with its peeling adobe and rusting truck parts and junk scattered around the yard. Priam outside lying in the hammock or sitting in a rocker that no longer rocked, wearing down the day, crabbing about the heat, cussing the dog or kicking the cat, whatever had the misfortune to cross his path, while a few dusty chickens pecked at what they could come by among the weeds.

One day after a cloudburst had turned the yard to mud, a beat-up black truck pulled into the ruts at the edge of the place, and a fellow unfolded himself from inside and made his way around the mud over to where Priam was sitting under the box elder, the only shade. A scrawny fellow with a high forehead, cleft chin, and a snaggletooth when he grinned, he stuck out a bony hand to offer a handshake and said, "Howdy, I'm Tiger Higgins, and I hear you own that piece of property there across the blacktop."

Priam looked him up and down. "What's it to you?"

"I got a business proposition—that's what."

"Prime land. Make you a fortune in the cattle business," Priam fired back. "I been waiting for the right investment."

"Looks to me like a grasshopper would starve over there. But I'll make you an offer you can't refuse."

I could tell Priam didn't believe a word of it, but the smell of a deal set his juices flowing. After a session of jawing and jockeying, sweating and swearing, the two of them landed in roughly the same spot, and afterward Priam even offered the fellow a shot of whiskey. Money changing from somebody's palm into his own always pumped him up for at least three days.

After two weeks of feverish activity—tearing out rotted posts and boards, hammering and nailing, repairing sheds and fence-posts, putting in metal bars and attaching chain-link fence—the place looked pretty good. Then a sign went up: ROADSIDE ZOO— ANIMALS FROM THE WILD. EXOTIC. THRILLING. THE JUNGLE BROUGHT TO YOUR VERY DOORSTEP.

The jungle—in the midst of that stretch of yucca and cactus and mesquite. The idea seized hold of my imagination—the biggest thing to happen to me since third grade. Once I'd learned to read and do arithmetic, Priam figured I had all the learning I would ever need to make my way in the world. The rest you could get from the TV—though ours offered mostly snow and static. Meanwhile he'd find enough to keep me busy.

I wanted to hang around and watch the goings-on—and a couple of times Tiger let me hand him nails and tools—fun stuff—while he told me about tracking animals and how you had to show the big cats who was boss. But after a couple of days Priam came and fetched me home.

"He ain't open yet, Missy—you can do a look-see later on." So I watched from the other side, when I wasn't taking care of the chickens or sneaking off to the arroyo to look for rocks with fossils on them. I'd found a neat book once in the school library showing creatures that had once lived when the world was new and the mountains were the bottom of the sea.

One day I got to go over and pick up the beer cans and whiskey bottles and paper cups and pieces of plastic that had been tossed out from passing cars. Tiger paid me a dollar and a half and gave me a soda. The place was beginning to look halfway decent.

The next day a big trailer-truck pulled up. Tiger and a couple of helpers, a high-school kid—big square fellow, Greg—and the other, Ralph—older but strong, who acted like he knew about animals—opened up the back and started unloading cages and crates, leading out the animals. They hefted a cage with a tiger onto a trolley, then another, with a young one, hardly more than a kit. I'd never seen a real live tiger before, never seen wild animals up close. And here came a leopard, an ocelot, a cougar. I got goose bumps all down my arms.

Then came the dog types—coyote, fox, and dingo. Some of the animals were new to me—I had to learn what they were. They led a camel into the yard, who passed it over with a sneer. I could see monkeys, even a zebra. There were birds too. A couple of gaudy parrots, and a big white cockatoo. Finally some wooden crates labeled *reptiles*.

Lights had been strung up along with the signs. GRAND OPENING. SPECIAL FAMILY RATE—LITTLE KINDS FREE. For a while things were hopping. People pulling in to look at the zoo would stop at the stand to buy a soda, some chips or popcorn or get a bag of food for the animals. 'You get folks involved—" Tiger said, "Keeps down the overhead that way." He tapped his head to show how full it was of smarts.

When the place closed up for the day, Tiger came over with a bottle of whiskey, and he and Priam poured it into two orange juice glasses and lifted them to the future. Tiger had a gold mine, nothing less, and he was full of plans now that he was on his feet again. Bad luck a while back with some of his animals over in Oklahoma. But he'd bought up a new supply from two zoos selling off their surplus and their elders. Now he was going to breed tigers again—he was waiting for the young female to get to where he could breed her. Once he'd bred over twenty tigers—that's how he'd got his name— and sold them all to folks that practically stood in line for one of the kits. A huge market for all he could produce. "You can't imagine—all the folks wanting their own tigers and ocelots and leopards, but especially tigers." He was one big cockeyed grin, and the two of them kept at that bottle till they were chummy as blood brothers.

After I'd nagged him till he was ready to tear his hair or mine, Priam took me over to see the animals. The cages were all lined up, the cats all together, the monkeys in their own spot, and the coyote, fox, and dingo in theirs. It was the little tiger that won my heart. I stood in front of her until I could feel Priam's impatience coming at me in a hot blast.

I hated to leave her. She just sat there looking around, bewildered, uncertain, like she'd found herself in a strange place and didn't know what to do. I could tell from her eyes.

The other cats acted like they knew exactly where they were and kept pacing from one end of their cages to the other. No wonder. There was hardly enough room for them to turn around. The lion was in a different space—didn't budge all the time we were there, just lay in the sun with his eyes half-lidded.

More action with the monkeys. They were moving all the time. Each had a swing, but they couldn't swing very far, so they took to hanging and swinging all along the sides. The parrots sat on their perches picking at their feathers. Every once in a while the cockatoo let out an ear-splitting shriek.

"Let's go home," I said. My head was full of noise and smells, and I had a sinking feeling I couldn't name.

"Now hold on," Priam said. "You had ants in your pants to get over here. And I got to see to my investment. I want a look at what's inside."

Inside were the reptiles, with a slimy smell. A big turtle sat on a little pile of dirt in a circle of stones, a pan of water nearby. To keep it company a pair of rattlers were draped over a dead branch nearby. Then in the next tank I saw a circle of thick coils spiraled around until they pointed forward into a dark head with a white stripe in the middle. The coils had wiggly black and yellow strips that made a pattern. Beautiful to look at, but it made me dizzy and sent chills down my spine. I held my breath.

"That's a python," Ralph said as he was setting things up. He'd just finished putting a heating pad under the tank. "Carpet python. How'd you like that for a pet?"

I could feel something coming from inside that python that nobody could claim. Different from the cats. I felt I knew them as soon as I laid eyes on them—their fierceness. Proud. Dangerous. I had the feeling they knew how to dream. I wanted to get to know the cats. I wasn't sure about the snakes. The python just fixed me to the spot, not giving anything away. Looked like it was curled around something calm but cold, like nothing would dare to bother it. Made me feel how jittery I was.

"If they trust you, they're easy to handle," Ralph said, maybe to reassure me. "Only you have to be careful. If they're hungry, they'll strike at anything that moves and throw their coils. The big ones can kill a man."

He would have gone on talking about them, but Priam hauled me off so that Tiger could show us the rest of his critters, as he called them. We threaded through the kids with their popcorn and sodas and bags of animal food, and their moms and dads. But I'd seen all I wanted, and kept pulling at Priam's arm till he was ready to slap me. "Go on home then," Priam said. "You make me tired."

"Wait a minute," Tiger said. "Come on over here. We'll give you a treat." He led us up to the soft drink stand and asked me what I wanted. "This one's on me."

I didn't want anything, but something told me I shouldn't say *no*. We stood for a moment watching the big kid I'd seen before, who stood behind the counter trying to add things up and make change for a family who'd bought drinks and popcorn and animal food. He was having a slow time of it.

When they left and I'd settled on a root beer, Tiger and Priam stepped back out the way to talk, while I watched one of the spider monkeys picking lice from his partner, and pretended I wasn't paying any attention to the men. But I always kept my ears cocked—learned a few things that way.

"Be good for her—give her something to do. Instead of being a plain damned nuisance."

"Pretty young to be putting money in her hands."

"She's a whiz, I tell you. Can make change like a cash machine. And that kid you got there running things . . . not too swift up there in the cockpit. Probably stealing from you on the sly. And come September . . ."

That's how I got my first job.

"Get you used to earning your way in the world," Priam told me. "Pay for your board and keep. It's owing to me right enough—all I've had to put up with." He made a face like he had an ache with nothing to cure it, and I went off to work a picture puzzle the social worker gave me before she moved away.

I was good at fishing out the sodas from the ice chest and filling the little packets of bread crumbs and bags of limp lettuce and vegetable tops and fruit Tiger collected free from the groceries to sell to folks that wanted to feed the animals. And I was good at making change. I got to keep two dollars of it every week after Priam took his cut. I put it in a little purse I had, to keep it from the damp, and hid it down near the arroyo under a special rock.

Things were pretty busy that summer. People pulling in to see the jungle at their doorstep. And, since it was hot and dusty, they bought lots of sodas. I liked talking to people and hearing where they came from, and I'd look at the kids and try to imagine how it was to go traveling with moms who wore lipstick and carried shiny purses and tall, good-looking dads, mostly with nice teeth, friendly smiles, and cameras hanging around their necks.

When nobody was around, I'd go visit the animals because none of us had anything much to do. And Ralph would tell me stories about them. He'd worked a lot with elephants and big cats, and he'd take me on his rounds and tell me about his days traveling with a circus.

"That's really exciting," I said, ready to be excited by just about anything.

"It was an interesting life," he said. "I liked being around the animals, especially the elephants. You get close to them. But I sure didn't like the way they were treated. They can be awful cruel in the way they train animals in some of those big circuses. The

20

trainers showing off for the public." He let me take that in.

Of course, I'd never seen a circus, and it sounded like a whole other world. It sounded like something magical.

"Animals have a lot to offer," he said. "If you listen, they'll tell you things. I swear it." I was ready to try for it.

Sometimes he was all jittery, complaining about Tiger and the zoo set-up. Too crowded. And Tiger was skimping on the food. "Those guys—I don't understand them. Why aren't they in real estate? They don't know what the hell they're doing. You think they care anything about what's sitting inside those cages?"

I tried to keep my eyes open to see how the animals were doing. The little tiger always looked glad to see me. They didn't have regular names—just a label like *Bengal Tiger* with a piece of Latin underneath. I tried to get to know the animals. I started talking to them, and it seemed like they were listening. Sometimes I'd sit real still and go over a bunch of names in my mind and see what came to me; then I'd try out different names on them. Gave me something to think about. I could tell the big male tiger liked *Caruso*, even though I tried *Hercules* and *Elvis*.

It took a long time to get to know the kit. Ralph liked to wrestle with her, just play with her like any cat. And he let me play with her too. I loved her. But mostly she was in her own space and a lot of the time seemed to be thinking or dreaming. At first I thought she was like a fairy princess who'd been stolen away from her land and home and turned into a tiger that had to wander for years till she was rescued from the wicked magician who'd betrayed her. But then Ralph told me she came from somebody's apartment, where she sometimes slept in her owner's bed. It seemed more like she'd forgotten how to be a tiger. I called her *Antoinette*.

"That's just right," Ralph told me. "She's lively and lovely—and that's what it sounds like. They need names—lets them know who they are," then he muttered to himself, "which is a hell of a lot more than some people know."

He gave Antoinette a stuffed owl to bat around. She lay on her back, holding it in her paws and raked it with her hind feet. "Disemboweling her prey," Ralph said. I knew what he meant. The owl didn't last long. Ralph put in a couple of cardboard boxes, and she had great fun leaping into them and sitting there like she'd found her spot. Sometimes he'd take her out on a leash and let her walk around. He'd let me hold onto it. He was careful though—didn't want me getting clawed or bitten.

"They don't mean to be rough, but they got claws and teeth. They're ruthless, cats are, even the domestic ones. I figure they're thinking all the time about the bird or the mouse they're going to catch. Only that's not all of it," he went on. "They can be affectionate, too. And everything they do is beautiful. Just watch how they move, how they sleep—in curves. All of them. Beauty and grace and playfulness—all of it together make them what they are—*cat*." He looked at me. Yes, *cat*. "Think of that." It really struck me, what he said, like he'd put something in front of me that was missing from my life and that I'd have to discover. Even though I couldn't really speak to it or know what it meant, I did try to be on the lookout for it. Even in our old tomcat, Hank.

The tigers were a big draw at the zoo, but it must have been hard just lying around with nothing to do except let people gawk at you. I could at least roam around a bit. And Ralph kept saying, "I got to get out of this place." The way things were going, I could see how it was getting to him. I couldn't think of anything to say that would help matters.

On the animal side, the camel was maybe doing the best, though I knew his legs were bothering him from arthritis, just like Priam's, and he was feeling droopy and irritable. He'd sit for long hours in the sun with his legs folded under him. I came up close just once, and he gave me a look as if to say, "Don't even bother." He looked like he was going to spit. Ralph never let the kids on his back—just on the burro and the Shetland—and that was a good thing.

In the afternoon the yard was blazing hot. And even the projecting roof boards of the stalls didn't help much. The animals just kept pacing till they'd had enough. Then they flopped down and shut their eyes and slept and kept on sleeping.

They didn't eat much either. Most of the stuff Tiger collected from restaurants and groceries was fit only for the crows, and Ralph would throw half of it away. Then one morning when Ralph gave Tiger a piece of his mind, the two of them started yelling at one another, and the way Tiger was waving his fist, I was afraid they were going to duke it out. But suddenly Ralph got all quiet, kind of dangerous looking, and turned and stalked off. "Asshole," he muttered, and shot Tiger a nasty look over his shoulder. He didn't show up for a couple of days, and I worried about him. Having to do all the work himself, Tiger was furious.

He jumped all over Ralph when he finally turned up "Where the hell have you been? Are you working here or not? I oughta fire you."

"Just go right ahead," Ralph challenged him. "What'll you do then? I'm only here on account of the animals."

"What d'you mean? I've given you a chance. Who else would give you a job?"

The rest of the afternoon Ralph was dark and angry and just glared ahead and wouldn't answer when I spoke to him. I had to work to keep back the tears.

Then he saw my face and grabbed me up in a hug. "Oh, I'm so sorry, sweetheart. Do forgive me. It isn't anything you've done. Just me and my bad mood." Then he hugged me again. "You're my best girl—always." Then I couldn't hold back.

Because I had to do something, I took some of my money and bought hamburger to give to Antoinette and Caruso. Then, because it wasn't fair to the others, I saved up and bought enough cheap hamburger to give all the cats and dogs a treat. The meat they were getting wasn't all that much and not all that good. A lot of chicken near the end of its career, and scraps of beef or pork the butcher had trimmed away—some of it starting to smell. Caruso would sniff it and stand there of two minds. If he was hungry enough he'd eat it. He was getting thin. Sometimes he'd sit and pull out pieces of his fur. "You're too beautiful to do that," I told him. "Please listen."

23

"It's a crying shame," Ralph said. "He earns a living off their backs, and he treats them like dirt. All cooped up in that little space. At least give them a good feed. Give 'em good meat and plenty of it. Horsemeat to fatten them up. Ever hear a big tiger purr? Like a motorboat."

The animals took hold of me. I knew how unhappy they were. I couldn't stop thinking about them. I carried them on my shoulders like a weight of bricks. They padded into my dreams and roared and bellowed. They scratched and bit and clawed each other. Their fierceness was sharp as hot needles that drove into their own hides. I could hardly stand it.

"The animals are getting sick," I told Priam.

"Well, Miss Smartie Pants, they oughta put you in charge, you know so much."

What can I do? I asked them. *Set us free*, they pleaded. Their cages were all locked up. But just suppose they were let out. What would happen then? They seemed to sink back deeper into their bodies as though they wanted to forget they were alive. The dingo, coyote, and fox were so thin you could count their ribs. By the end of the summer, the parrots had plucked out so many feathers they looked scruffy as old carpet and sat on their perches like they'd been stuffed. All their spirit had leaked away into the air— whatever they had had of beauty and grace.

Tiger himself seemed to be losing his grip. You'd see him one moment, and then he'd disappear, taking off in the middle of the afternoon, leaving everything to Ralph and me. He wouldn't show up till after Ralph closed the place up for the day. Then he'd slouch in to count up "the proceeds," as he called them, add up every dime, frown as he paid us once a week, put the rest into his wallet and march off. Some days he looked at us like we were to blame for the thin pickings. Maybe he thought we were stealing. One afternoon when nobody was around, I found Ralph among the reptiles, taking the python out of his tank. He put it around his shoulders and let it crawl down his chest. I sucked in my breath. I wasn't sure what to think about it.

"You want to try?"

I wasn't sure, but something in me wanted to do it.

"I bet you don't scare easy," he said. "You can do it. You don't want to startle them. They got to trust you."

I had to look around inside for a quiet spot. I took a couple of deep breaths, and then Ralph lifted the snake up to my shoulders and it came on around. It was an odd feeling at first, something like that crawling on me. It wasn't slimy at all, more silky. At first I held still as a tree trunk. Then I held out my arm and the python came down my arm and around my waist. I was tingling all over, and I felt happy too. Ralph grinned at me. It was like I'd passed some kind of test.

"You like that, huh? They don't take much bother, but you got to keep them at the right temperature. Neither cook them or let them freeze."

I was hardly listening. I was replaying all the sensations, knowing there was fear still there, a dark place beyond anything I knew. And something else—different, but I couldn't say what it was.

It seemed like his mood had changed, as though he was trying to give me the best of himself. I spent time with him whenever I could, helping him feed and water the animals, so I could hear his stories.

The last one he told me lay closest to his heart—about the one circus he loved, where he handled a half-grown elephant named Tillie. A small outfit in Missouri with only one ring—"a glorious circus," he told me, as he described the acrobats, the Cossack riders and their feats of horsemanship, the Flying Wonders on the high wire, the jugglers and clowns, and Lola, who rode the elephant. A whole parade leapt up before my eyes. It was like I was there. And the more he described, the more I wanted to be in their midst.

"Color and lights and music," he said. "Skill and daring. Think of putting yourself out there—taking the risks in spite of all the dangers—plus bad days and small audiences . . ."

I'd never seen him so excited. His eyes lit up. His forehead glowed. Even his bald spot gave off a special shine.

"They were the best—one big family," he said.

"Why did you leave?"

"Like I told you," he said, "it was a small outfit. They did things on a shoestring. Then too much competition—TV, films, sports. They had ten good years. And those were the best of my life."

After that I never heard Ralph complain. He just kept things to himself and did his rounds like a robot. He got a bad cough, bronchitis, and was gone for more than a week. I really worried about him and about the animals. Tiger again had all the work to do himself. He needed help, especially with the cats and brought in some guy who acted like the whole place was a bad scene and quit after three days.

Tiger had a distracted look. Now there were times when he let the water bowls go foul or empty, and I'd drag out the hose and try to get water to the animals. Since he knew I was doing it, he just let everything drop into my hands.

The animals kept visiting me at night—pacing up and down. *This is a prison,* Caruso groaned. *We're dying here.* In my dream I did my best to comfort them. *When I grow up, I'll bring you all home and give you good food, and there'll be lots of room where you can run and be free.* It was no use. *We are dying into our freedom.* I'd wake up breathless and scared, but I didn't know what to do. Once I sat up yelling. The animals were lying all around me in scraps and pieces. I could hardly recognize them.

"Some of the animals aren't doing well," I said to Tiger.

"They think they got privileges," he snapped. "Full of themselves—that's what, just because they perform for the public. Never saw an animal yet that didn't want to up its standard of living." He strode off, muttering. "They think they got troubles." One of the troubles he probably wasn't expecting was a big dark-haired woman, who pulled in one afternoon and stood over me like a tower, then spoke out in a deep voice that had no nonsense in it. "What are you doing here, child, and who runs this outfit?"

I could hardly find my voice. "Mr. Tiger Higgins." "And where is this Tiger person?"

26

"I believe he went into town, Ma'am."

"And left you here by yourself? Outrageous." She wrote something in a notebook she was carrying.

Since school was in full swing and hardly anybody was coming in, Tiger left me in charge when he went off in the afternoons. Ralph came in when he felt up to it, but he wasn't working whole days. Often Tiger brought back the smell of where he'd been, and I didn't want to get near him. "Just tell anybody looking for me that your dad's gone to town for supplies," he told me, "and he'll be back in a jiffy."

I didn't want to tell that kind of lie. And I couldn't have told it to her. She didn't offer to buy a ticket, but started walking around among the cages, inspecting the place and writing things down. "And what's your name, honey?" she said, when she came back.

I didn't want to tell her everybody called me *Missy*, even when I'd gone to school. And I'd left behind my paper name that nobody ever used. Something struck me though. I had named the tigers and the other animals, all except the python—I wasn't sure about his yet—why couldn't I name myself? I could call myself anything I wanted. It struck just then what exactly I did want.

"Grace," I said. "My name's Grace." And even as I said it, I knew it was a secret thing, and I'd be telling it only at the right moment.

"It's a good name," she said, looking me over. She started to say something, then just muttered, "the jackass." She put a card down on the counter and said, "Give this to your Mr. Tiger." Then she put away her notebook. "Well, darling, with a name like that I'll bet you'll break out of whatever cage you happen to land in. Just you remember that." Then she was gone.

I spent the rest of the afternoon mooning and dreaming, trying to figure out what she meant.

Ralph came in late that afternoon. "Any visitors?" he said.

"Not really." I handed him the card she'd left.

"He can't say I didn't warn him."

I knew in my bones it was all coming to an end—that Ralph

would move on, leaving a great hole in my life. At one point I guessed that he had been in trouble somewhere along the line, perhaps had come to the zoo looking for refuge. But I never had any desire to smoke it out. What mattered was what he gave me, though it was a long time before I caught on to its real dimensions. He'd led me toward my name—that much was clear. But at the same time he revealed for me a path through the jungle—where I could take my wildness.

THE HOUSE ON THE LAKE

When Isabelle came to take possession of the house she'd inherited, she had the eerie feeling that it was already inhabited. She kept waking in the middle of the night to sounds that could have been the scraping of a chair or footsteps in the hallway or across a room. Her heart pounding, she would get up to investigate, creeping along the wall outside her bedroom to listen, afraid she might actually come upon an intruder. She found no such evidence, but she was not appeased. Could someone have crept in and kept hidden during the daylight hours and become an elusive presence at night? Was the house pregnant with memories that wouldn't sleep? Or was it simply her nerves?

Everything about the house seemed unreal, most of all the way it had come into her possession. She'd seen Andre, her stepfather, in a hospital in Lausanne just before he died—shrunken, skeletal, embittered over the way life had treated him as he'd knocked about from pillar to post. Cheated, in other words. No mention of a house. Then, a year or so later, she'd been summoned to a lawyer's office in Geneva to receive the deed to a house she'd inherited from her father. But it wasn't Andre's name on the deed, nor that of her real father, whom she hadn't seen in some years—a distant figure of her youth who'd sent her money while she was at the Sorbonne. He had helped her during a difficult period, and there had been a few intermittent phone calls and letters, but they had rarely seen one another. She stared at the signature of her benefactor and levied a barrage of questions. But the lawyer patiently repeated that her father had given instructions that she was to have the house. She was handed a deed, keys, directions, and the phone number of the caretaker.

From the moment she arrived, Isabelle experienced, first, astonishment: Who could have built such a dwelling? Could it be that Andre's mining ventures in Bolivia or Peru or Zimbabwe—wherever he'd been lured by the promise of instant wealth—had panned out? Was it his closely held secret—a wish to surprise and mystify her—in keeping with his sense of irony? But he was too much of an egoist not to want to parade his largesse. When her astonishment had subsided, she felt something close to anguish. It was too much, far too much. More than she deserved, or perhaps more than she'd bargained for. She'd arrived to take possession— of what exactly? What sort of life could she live here, grafted onto what she saw as hopelessly twisted branches? The view of the lake, Lago Maggiori, near the Italian border—how could she quarrel with this sheer beauty? The house itself was a stunning marriage of location and design, wealth and imagination. It would be all she could do to keep it up and pay the taxes.

She opened the gate to a garden at its peak. One bed held roses of every hue and description. In others were flowers that ranged from the palest blue to deepest purple, a vine of passion flowers clinging to the wall. Palm trees, so unexpected in that alpine region, as well as agaves, one in perfect bloom, rose above the color below. The granddaddy of prickly pears claimed both corners of the wall leading up to the doorway. Elephant ears and birds of paradise. It was not just variety and the explosion of color that took her eye, but the little walks and steps that took you to different prospects of lake and garden. Sculptures that you could walk through and around, columns and shapes, a little bridge that children would have delighted in. Not only a sense of beauty had been at work, but a kind of playfulness. Some of the forms had been left unfinished, as if they required further inspiration. A little maze led to the pond in the center, shaped like an eye, orange captured in a ring of lazily circling goldfish. When she drew nearer she saw that the center, the pupil, held water flowing over varying colors of glass. She stood mesmerized until finally she had to draw back or lose herself in its depths.

She caught her breath. What wizardry had created all this? Who was her father after all? She shook herself back into practicality and returned to the car for the groceries and the case of wine she'd bought in Lugano. She set them down to open the door. Her cat, Lily, followed her in.

In the entryway she met a towering golden Buddha that looked down on her with a serenity that made her fidget. In its company was a dancing Shiva. Though she wanted to cling to the notion, it was difficult to think of Andre on any terms with these deities, unless something had figured into his last years. He had lived on his own terms, insisting on his particular truth to the point of what madness? Oh, but she'd adored him when she was little! And she'd always had a soft spot for him, admired his sense of independence, his daring. She wanted to strike from the record that last vision of him as he lay dying.

She paused for a moment on the upper balcony past the entry way and glanced at the shelves of books that extended all along the balcony and took a brief survey: history, philosophy, drama, poetry, art. Andre had been well educated, but she saw him as too much of a rolling stone to collect a library. She'd lost track of him during the unsettled period following their return to Europe and her mother's divorce. That was the era of ruined possibilities. They'd established contact after she was on her own, and would have dinner together when they were both in Paris—in his case, not often. But he had called for her during his last illness.

More books in the study, where the windows, she saw, were open. That gave her a start. But she herself had arranged with the caretaker to open up the house for her. He had removed the dust covers and prepared it to be lived in. Books and papers lay about the desk, as though someone had paused in the midst of his labors and would return to his work soon—a clue perhaps that might lead her to the hidden genius of the house, that is when she could take time from all the details that filled her days: getting telephone, gas, and water connected, arranging for a new line for her computer, learning the domestic arrangements, and finally meeting the caretaker, Paolo, who presented her with an African grey parrot. "A great friend of your father's," he said.

"Cesario. He speaks very well—they used to have conversations. Only now he doesn't talk." He paused. "Grief—that is my impression. I have kept him since . . ."

"Do you think he'll speak again?" she asked. She could imagine Andre with a parrot, the first real suggestion that the house might have been his.

'When he is ready. I play music for him. He sways to the music. And he likes to survey the garden from this perch."

The parrot looked at her as though to size her up, tilted his head, and took up residence on the perch.

"A great man, your father. He spent a lot of time here, together with Antonio, planting, installing the sculptures with the workmen. He was full of plans for that plot on the other side of the house."

In the days that followed, Isabelle tried to follow Paolo's instructions for taking care of the bird and to make sure there was no threat from Lily. She made some efforts to coax it to speak, but, though it didn't appear unfriendly, it gave her no encouragement. She had the sense she had been led into absurdity and challenged by some standard impossible to meet. Outside influences seemed still to be at work shaping the space. Was she being watched? She was like her cat, ears cocked for the slightest sound, listening, pausing in the midst of whatever she was doing to catch a sound from upstairs that suggested a presence.

From the papers and books that littered the desk in the study she could imagine someone in the midst of a literary undertaking. She picked up fragments written on scraps of paper. "But consider me in all this," she read. "What is there but ruin and loss?"

Whose voice was this? Andre's, her mother's, her father's? She considered a moment—or hers? On another: "Is the notion of happiness itself an illusion? What is to be sought—is it worth the seeking?" On the third evening of her tentative ownership, she could have sworn that a certain book lying on the desk had not been there before, or else had been open to a different page. *Lost Worlds,* she read in blue letters on the spine.

The writer of the book spoke with passionate conviction about a vanished race lost thousands of years ago when a whole continent had blown apart and sunk to the depths of the Pacific. Home of the highest civilization ever known to have existed. He described a race of towering presences not yet materialized into human shape, who could communicate telepathically and whose sensibilities gave them an intimate entry into the inner lives of animals, trees, and plants, down to the very stones. Consider the subjectivity of a flower or a stone, the writer suggested. Sentences were marked, underlined. Comments dotted the margins. "How far beyond us," she read, after a description of their artistic and spiritual achieve ments. She bent to pick up a scrap of paper that had fallen to the floor. "What the imagination once created—can it again come into being? Is it ever lost?"

Imagination indeed. She'd never heard of such a place. Its rem- nants, she read, were still to be in found in the Hawaiian Islands, fragments left behind from the great explosion that sent this civil ization to the ocean's depths.

She was thunderstruck. Was this evidence of Andre's old pas- sion—what had triggered his uprooting them all and taking them to Tahiti, supposedly to disprove Thor Heyerdahl's theory that the ancient Egyptians had come originally from the South Seas? The pretext for a quixotic search for a lost paradise? She closed the book. The room suddenly seemed to dissolve into an indetermi- nate space that could hold any possibility—as though what could be imagined could, with enough passion, take form. She could almost see the forest dwellings where this exalted race lived and schooled their young so that they would reach the highest levels of development in complete harmony with the universe.

Paradise. The golden time that lived in the common dream. Thanks to Andre she'd known such a time—that remarkable year of her childhood, when they'd sublet their apartment, left behind their friends and relatives in Paris, who thought they were out of their minds, and gone to Tahiti. There standing before her was Edwina Dawkins under her sun hat, her horsey face pale with blotchy red skin, always in need of protection from the sun. "Now, my dears," she was saying, "tomorrow we'll go off to the Tuamutu Islands and do our hunting." With the parrot feathers on her straw hat, together with her great beak of a nose, she was transformed into a giant predatory bird. "If only we could find a Gloriamaris or an Excelsus. Or even a Gaughini." Her great dream. Had she ever found any of those or other rarities? Isabelle wondered.

She and Martin, Dan and Maria, Tommy, and don't forget doll-like Nancy, were wild with enthusiasm for what the day promised. All of them in Miss Dawkins's charge. They were Isabelle's family, teasing, playing tag, racing one another into the waves, tumbling in the sand like puppies. The delicious freedom of it. The space around her became the beach, and once again she was romping along the skirt of the ocean.

During the day they swam and explored. Come nightfall they took up kerosene lanterns and combed the beach. Their lamps drew up another life, otherwise hidden creatures emerging from the sand only to be popped into the sacks they carried. They took their treasure to Miss Dawkins, who put the creatures into slatted boxes and, with the help of the boys, buried them in the sand. A month later they returned to dig them up. Carnivorous ants had eaten away the flesh of the creatures inside, and the shells, clean and shining, were for sale in the shops of Tahiti or back in England. "Hold them up to your ear for the sound of the sea inside," Miss Dawkins invited them. They all heard the subdued roar. Isabelle cherished a box of the shells Miss Dawkins had allowed her to keep. She had it with her still.

At the time she harbored a secret fear her mother might ask where they'd been or what they'd been up to during those days Miss Dawkins took them off to the islands 400 sea miles from Tahiti to search for what would become shells. What would her mother or Andre have thought of their sea baths among eels (since there was no fresh water)? Would they have been shocked to see their children covered in some tarry substance, a cleaning solution probably known only to the British? As far as she knew, none of the children under Miss Dawkins's care spoke to outsiders of their adventures. Perhaps even then they knew they had hold of something unique. She needn't have worried—her mother had been much too absorbed in her painting to fret about what the children might be doing.

The buzzer from the front gate brought Isabelle back to more pressing matters, a letter she had to sign for. She expected some legal matter, but saw to her surprise it was from her daughter, Aimee. "I hear you've struck it rich," she read. How had she come by such nonsense? But waiting under the words was the giddy sense of opportunity to be snatched. "So I'm going to offer you an opportunity to be a real mother to me. I want to go into business." Business? When Aimee had no sense of money? What now? Isabelle wondered. "I have a chance to buy into a shop that sells body products. I want to create a new life." She then asked for a sum that made Isabelle gasp. Was she back on drugs, she wondered, and, with something like despair, she tried to picture what state Aimee was in at the moment. Repeating, it seemed, her own troubled youth—trips to Amsterdam, flinging herself into the drug scene there and elsewhere, lost outside of *memory*. It was out of all this that Aimee had emerged into the world.

She put Aimee's letter aside, her mind a jumble of conflicting impulses about how she should respond, or whether she should respond at all. She was in need of distraction. She took a brief walk along the lake, then threw herself into a graphics project she had contracted for. She had set up her computer downstairs on a table in the kitchen, unable as yet to establish herself in the study. The sun was gone when she finally emerged, exhausted. She poured a glass of wine, then sat for a long time watching the mountains fade into the evening. The lake grew dark.

The darkness cut her off, created a wall, presenting her with her loneliness. She went into the kitchen to prepare pasta. She would be eating alone now and for how long? Mealtimes were always the most difficult—that pause when food and wine demanded the presence of others, the pleasure of conversation and company. She pushed aside the plate and went to phone her step-sister, Elise—a call long overdue. She would *try* to make it up to her. She had to talk to her about the house, the father they had shared. The phone rang, but there was no answer. She left a message and turned away disappointed.

She had difficulty sleeping. But, when she finally drifted off, she dreamt of a city of astonishing beauty. Its dwellings rose into crystal palaces and colors played within them. Better than Oz, more spectacular than Shanghai. Beyond compare. Occupied by presences continually revealing themselves in forms of thought, perhaps dreamers themselves in the midst of creating their own reality.

She woke to mist—the lake and sky merged into one, offering a disorienting sense of where she was. After coffee and a cigarette had returned her to the realm of the ordinary, she roamed the house adjusting a vase here, a throw rug there. Nothing of this belonged to her, but *every* item revealed a taste and appreciation that invited her to further discernment. She was avoiding the study, for fear she would be met by some new and unsettling offering. Finally she had to enter, and there she found Andre waiting.

He was running along the beach, a letter in his hand, and shouting joyfully, "I'm ruined! I'm ruined!" They'd been getting a monthly stipend from Jacques, Andre's former brother-in-law, who had agreed to run the factory while Andre was away. Now here was the letter, no stipend enclosed, announcing that Andre was no longer owner of the factory. By some law peculiar to France, the business had become forfeit because Andre had been away for more than a year. It now belonged to Jacques, who had seized his opportunity.

Ironically, it was the escape Andre had been waiting for. He'd inherited the family business, manufacturing a brand of biscuits and butter cookies known throughout Europe. Though doing business was not in his temperament, he had greatly increased its sales. Perhaps one of the attractions he'd offered her mother was the living he provided. She had a taste for elegant surroundings and designer clothes, Lancome perfumes, and foie gras. But now that Andre was unleashed, free not to return, he was bursting with new ideas. He could build boats, hire out as captain for tourists. Isabelle's mother could continue to paint. "Think of the life we could build here. The mountains, the beach, life in the sun. The best champagne at the cheapest price. You could never starve here—wild fruits, fish . . . Paradise."

There began the first of their many quarrels.

"Listen," her mother said, "even Gauguin had to invent his paradise. We'd already brought in the syphilis that killed him. I'm a European," she insisted, "for better or worse. I'm not here to repeat his efforts to escape civilization—it's already beaten us here. All right, so it's corrupt, but at least it's a corruption I understand. Money, I like it." She made a gesture of running bills through her fingers.

The air in the study was filled with accusation and outrage. Raw. Snakes hissing, dogs at one another's throats. Andre waving his arms, her mother screaming at him. Money, money. She had a child to support. Isabelle stood before them offering up her little embroidered purse. Even now the field was darkened and rage poured through it. When had he ever denied either of them? Nothing but the best. What were pockets for but to empty so that you could fill them again—with pleasure, with new adventures? He could have lived on breadfruit and mangoes, waiting for the next best chance. Ah, that lover of possibility. Isabelle felt a longing in his direction. He could go with the flow—what did up or down matter?

Would it have mattered that the local culture was being turned into a spectacle for tourists, with its display of Polynesian beauties for them to gawk at? What would he have done as more and more people poured in, pushing up the price of real estate, the cost of goods? "Even if he gets to the top of things one moment, he'll have lost it all in a poker game the next"—her mother's assessment. In the end he followed her mother back to Europe, then slipped away into gossip and legend while her mother resumed painting, made a place for herself in society, and married her third husband, a count who was entranced with her beauty. Isabelle was sent to live with her grandmother.

She was left to puzzle over Andre and his house. How could it possibly have been his?

"We had Paradise," he'd croaked at her from his deathbed, "and threw it away."

"I loved it all," she said. She could hardly tell him what it had meant to her, but the sense of it had shaped her, the sense of loss when they'd left. That space, original and unspoiled, before complexity had set in. She could not tell him of the longing it had induced. But he already knew.

"Precious one," he said, holding out his hand. "We are joined like . . ." A cough interrupted him. "You have . . . the whole world." He fell back—the words had taken all his effort. His face became blank, as though he were looking off toward what had so long eluded him.

But what did she have? The whole world? She fretted over the ambiguity he'd left her with, quite certain he'd had nothing to do with where she found herself. Her mother had gone off to Argentina with the count. Andre was dead. That left only her father, her mother's first husband.

If there was a path to discovery, she had the uneasy sense that it lay within the study. Inspite of herself she was drawn to it, intimidated by it, and yet, when she reached a place where her work flagged, she was impelled to go upstairs and enter, tentatively, the way Lily, her cat, entered a room. But Lily never entered this one.

Once again Isabelle was certain of a presence there. The book she had closed was lying open, this time to a page describing the mental life of the ancient race that had once existed. *Thought—if* that was what it should be called-quite beyond the mental experience of human beings. *Mind—the* five senses meeting and merging, finally leaping to a sixth, an antenna intuiting the whole fabric of existence.

Nothing of memory, just the forward pulsation of consciousness. Memory had come with man and his particular limitations—a creature of flesh after all. But those beings leapt into a reality that transcended mere form to become meaning. Isabelle seemed to stand on a chair looking through a keyhole into the realm of saints and mystics—quite beyond her.

Yet the vision didn't hold. The great crystal temples where the inhabitants entered to renew their creative lives and commune with the forces of the cosmos were there only for an instant. She was watching a sudden great explosion: the very planet shifted on its axis and, amid bubbling gases and moving plates, the continent broke up, the temples blown to smithereens—as though some jealous force had been lying in wait, as indeed it had. Another race, eagerly vying for power, had plotted to seize control.

She looked around in panic as the nightmare unfolded on the page. Inwardly fragmented, she wondered if there could ever be a condition other than war. That night and those that followed it, she woke in a sweat, darkness boiling up and invading her dreams. Was there a doom built into the heart of things, life continually at war with itself? What if there had indeed been a civilization beyond anything the world had known, beings capable of dreaming to the essential, to the very heart of stillness, to the energies of the dancing Shiva? But man, the latest arrival, had taken the lightning bolts into his own hands and flung them about with out mercy or reason. Ordinarily the newspaper accompanied her morning coffee and cigarette, however grim the news. Now she couldn't bear to look at it.

Though she hadn't followed her mother's path—her mother was beyond imitation—she had in secret shaped something of her mother's talent and made it her own. She'd done folders full of drawings, some of them with fanciful creatures on an island of her own invention. She carried these with her wherever she moved, neglecting them for long periods, then working on her drawings with feverish intensity. She hadn't touched them for a long time. In her troubled state she was impelled to take out her inks and colored pencils. On a weekend that stretched like a void in front of her, she unrolled a large sheet of drawing paper and began to draw, not knowing what would come. As she worked a vision opened up before her eyes of a great cataclysm—a gigantic flash, a progressive set of gaseous explosions in which the planet disintegrated, sending the seas into tsunamis and exploding mountains, rocketing men, women, children into space, heads and limbs torn apart and spewed out into the universe, where they might float forever. Caught up in her passion to set it all down on paper, as if the premonition remained apart from the catastrophe. Was there no residue of consciousness? Were all those eons of life creating itself totally extinguished? She worked late into the night, hardly conscious of what she was doing, until, numbed and exhausted, she threw herself into bed.

When she awakened to what she'd done, she couldn't bear to look at her creation. Quickly she rolled up the drawings and put them away. She knew what she had to do—sell the house and get out before she lost her mind. As soon as she had her coffee, she searched the telephone book for the names of realtors and called one for an appointment. What she would do once she wiped away the present, she had no clue. Suppose she simply set out by boat, train, plane, car, and spent the rest of her life hopping from one place to another, never looking back?

That morning she had a call from Elise. "Isabelle!" she said. "You're really back among the living?" Isabelle wasn't certain.

"When I heard your voice . . . I've been so worried. The letters all came back . . ."

'I'm sorry," Isabelle said. "I went into hiding—Aimee, the divorce . . ."

"I thought you'd fallen off the edge. You know, of course, about Papa."

"No," she said, knowing now.

"You didn't know," Elise said, in some confusion. "Not even with the house?"

"It wasn't in his name. I thought perhaps Andre was playing some sort of game."

"He changed it—legally. After he came back from India the last time."

"I don't understand."

"Something happened to him there. I can't tell you exactly, but it's like he woke up in a different skin. You can't imagine . . ."

"Do come," was all Isabelle could say.

"I can't leave the farm yet. My favorite horse—I may have to put him down."

'I'm sorry."

They spoke a bit longer. "I want to see you—and the house," said Elise. "It was incredible the way he put his whole life into *une idee fixe*. So many sketches. Nearly all his money. His dream, his passion, his retreat. He went there to write."

"Write what?"

"Poems, stories, essays. Words poured out of him. I still have some of his travel journals. He never showed them to anyone."

How strange it was. Even while they were speaking, the question kept nagging at her. Why had he wanted her to have the house, his creation? Elise was more daughter to him than she had ever been. He'd settled her in Normandy on the farm she'd wanted. What Isabelle remembered of him was the awkward shyness between them. He'd tried to get her to talk about what interested her: what was she reading? Was she enjoying her lectures? Actually she never finished. He gave her a painting for her room. She was surprised later to discover it was valuable. She had given it to her roommate. Something of her mother's contempt for him had infected her, and he lacked Andre's appeal.

Now she had to take him on, confront what he'd left her with. It was dismaying to reassess her relation to him, especially now that he wasn't there—and yet he was. She had, in effect, chosen not to be his daughter. Now, it appeared, he was waiting for their reunion. Prompted by something more than curiosity, she was trying to prepare herself to relinquish what she'd held onto for so long. Hadn't she really wanted Andre to be her father, to take her father's place? Perhaps it all lay in that year Andre had given her, when the life force had rushed so joyfully through her entire be-ing. When she hadn't had to give a thought to what Miss Daw-kins was doing when she sent out her little band of children to do her business. Or how it was for the creatures that lived in the shells to be devoured by ants. The innocence of her delight. Now her father had shoved Andre aside and come back to stake his claim, to haunt her.

She was angry about it. And when she went past the study the next morning she was almost in a rage.

"I hate mystery," she told the room. "I hate not knowing. I hate the idea of caring about you and what you did or didn't do with your life." She stood for a moment listening to the throb of her ill-feeling, and then to something like a sigh. Her own perhaps. Was there no escape?

She took a deep breath and stepped into the room. To her surprise, it was her mother who was waiting for her. She went to a rectan-gle she'd noticed between two bookshelves to see what lay behind the curtain that covered it. And there it was: the self-portrait of her mother that had struck like lightning into the midst of their lives. She studied it—it was not simply her own beauty her mother had captured, but something more fascinating, even fateful. No one could walk into a room without staring at her, being drawn to her. And yet it was a beauty too mercurial, too dazzling to hold onto. An enigma. Certainly Andre had been caught in the spell, as her father must have been.

The story had haunted her for years, how Andre on some busi-ness in her father's law office, where the portrait hung, had stood in front of it spellbound. "Who is this?" he demanded.

"My wife."

"But no longer," Andre murmured.

Had he heard, her father? Was there a response? Did he laugh and shrug it off? Tell the fellow he was an idiot? Didn't he have the balls to throw him out, or did he know he couldn't hold onto her? As for her mother, was she a mystery even to herself?

For it had happened exactly as Andre had spoken. To marry her, Andre had left behind a wife and three children.

Isabelle could remember nothing of their courtship. Perhaps it happened clandestinely. She'd been sent off to her grand mother's the day her parents had separated. When she returned, she remembered that the apartment was filled with flowers—from her father. He'd even left a meal for them. When he went to his bachelor digs, according to the story, there was a book of La Fontaine's fables open to one that applied directly to him, as well as a collection of poems by Bonnefoy, with certain lines marked:

> Farewell, our destinies were not the same.
> You must take this path and we the other,
> And between them grows deeper and denser
> That valley which the unknown looms over
> with the quick cry of the swooping bird of prey.

He'd been stripped of his domestic life. But with what passivity! Though he'd remarried a young widow who came to him with her daughter, Elise, their days together had been short-lived. Three years later he'd lost her to encephalitis. He did not remarry.

Isabelle began sorting through his papers. Apparently his wanderings began long after she had had contact with him. She read descriptions of various islands of the South Pacific she'd never heard of, where he'd located ruins that had to have been the works of higher civilizations—great carved faces, massive blocks of stones, moved who knew how. No one he encountered could explain their origins. "I lose myself in wandering," he wrote, "since there is nothing left to bind me—very little to lose, even my life."

Then on to India, Sikim, Nepal, Tibet. Looking for origins, perhaps, or relics.

She found a folder full of symbols that purported to describe the forces that once lay at the foundations of the lost world: trees and serpents, triangles and circles enclosed in a pair of triangles. She was unable to read the notes scribbled beside them. A name appeared farther on with various commentaries. Bits of conversation noted. A teacher or priest, it appeared, who claimed to be a descendant of those who survived the ancient catastrophe, those who'd fled to caves where they'd hidden, passing down their knowledge from one generation to the next.

These were notes apparently for a work-in-progress; and, as she read them through, she did not know if her father had intended a work of fiction or whether this was a transcription of an actual experience. She could hardly believe it. He called it a construct of contemplation. "I learned the sacred symbols of the creative energies that once belonged to us, how energy in its various particles is continually forming, reaching into infinity." Beckoning her to another space and time. She heard her cat meowing to be fed.

Beckoning her. She couldn't give it up now, however difficult she found it to live there. She didn't know if the house would ever be hers or if she could enter her father's life enough to know where he had gone. She would have to start with what was there, just as when she first entered, to reimagine its creation. She could envision the spot where he placed the house. The lake on one side and cliff on the other, its rocks jutting out. And he had accepted those rocks as a gift, incorporating them into the wall of the veranda little vines growing in the cracks that opened so expansively onto the lake. All part of the house now, but taking in water, mountains, sky. She had come to love sitting there in the evening looking out over the lake and the garden. Part of a Corinthian column stood at one side, with the figure of a youth beside it.

Her father had taken up those remnants of the past and reinstated them, those fragments of consciousness left from the explo sions of time. Like a curator he had sought to preserve the sensual loveliness of things: in the colors of the furniture and drapes, the paintings and tapestries, the ceramic pieces that decorated walls and tables in his music library. As though having been stripped of everything, he'd put together for himself not only a whole series of treasures, but also his efforts to create something out of them. These he had left to her. She was beginning to gain a sense of her inheritance. Perhaps he had chosen her, hoping to give her a platform from which something further might spring.

On the porch the parrot sat on its perch watching her. Would it ever speak? she wondered. Would she ever be able to commune with it? She imagined taking a feather with a strong quill tapering delicately at the feathery tip and dipping it into a bottle of ink.

SPIRIT OVER WATER

Now that Jade had embarked on her new venture, the house and porch had taken on the aspect of transition, that of people moving in or out. The porch was piled with furniture—bureaus and tables, chairs and chests, even an old wheelbarrow. On weekends and sometimes during the week, Jade drove off to estate sales and auctions, and returned in her battered truck with the treasures she'd acquired. From the beginning, Lavinia had her doubts. What did Jade know about refinishing furniture, and where would she sell it? She was convinced that her sister Maggie had allowed herself to be cajoled once again into another scheme that boded ill for the future.

Maggie, on the other hand, held her breath as she'd done each time Jade came back to gather her forces for a new foray into the world. How could she withhold her hope from her one chick, the next generation? This time it would be different, Jade assured her. She was through with men for one thing. Feckless and brutal and power hungry-walking egos with only their cocks to give them a sense of significance. And she was through with politics: the faction and delay, the meanness and self-interest. Let all that go too. Let the past be cut away like a bloody fragment.

This time she had put her faith and her muscle into a work of rescue, refinishing old furniture, restoring good wood to new life. Now she combed the newspapers for notices of auctions and yard sales. People had no idea what lay under the surface of old paint, ancient varnish. With a little imagination, think what could be done with chairs and tables with broken parts, marred surfaces. Just until she got back on her feet, Jade persuaded her, would Maggie give a little advance? Maggie juggled things as best she could. The house and yard would have to wait.

Two or three times a week, Jade came home, exultant and

eager. "See that table there—solid oak under that varnish. Just needs a little gluing and the leg replaced and those burn spots sanded off. I'll get triple for it. I paid only a hundred and a quarter."

A hundred and a quarter! How it all added up. Seventy-five here and fifty there. And God knows how much altogether. For Lavinia, it was all nonsense. The girl should go out and get herself a job. Not that she'd ever held one for very long. At one point Maggie said gently, "Don't you think you need to get some stuff in shape before you collect any more?"

That was not Jade's way of doing things. She had to reach a certain point of definition, a point that tipped from potential to actualization, the right moment when promise could be shaped and materialized, sent winging into the world. Then she would be ready to turn her energies toward it with all the furious ecstasy of a hummingbird in motion. Get it all done at once. She needed inventory. Think of how much you could sell just with impulse buying.

Maggie sighed inwardly. It wasn't that Jade lacked talent or energy or intention—she had always been able to see her potential. But once again she was being called upon for patience.

Hurricane Katrina was gathering force out in the Gulf, headed toward New Orleans. Katrina. What a distinction, Maggie thought, as she laid down the newspaper, for the Katrinas of the world named for a force of nature. She was pouring a second cup of coffee when the doorbell rang, and she opened the screen door to a young man, heavyset, pink-cheeked, head carefully shaved. It gave off a shine like the peak of an innate cheerfulness. He was from the city. The yard had to be mowed, he told her—there had been complaints from the neighbors— and the stuff removed from the front porch. This was, in fact, the second complaint from the neighbors, and she was violating ordnance no. 906A. The yard was not only unsightly, but it presented a health hazard. The grass was over four inches high.

47

"Ms. Mock," the young man said, "what are we going to do about this? We've got a problem here."

"Well, the grass just got out of hand. I've been out of commission for over a month now and . . ." She hardly knew how to explain. "My daughter has been collecting this furniture—it's her plan to refinish and sell it. We've got a garage in back. That's her workshop."

"You're not zoned for business. If she does the refinishing here and then sends it to a shop, that's something else."

"Yes, I see."

"But she'll have to get it off the porch, and something will have to be done about the yard."

Already the grass was too high just to mow. She'd had to let it go after the accident that had left her with a broken wrist and neck injuries. She'd collected insurance money—the driver had been drunk, but now her settlement was about to run out. Soon she hoped to get back to her work as a potter. She had her work in a craft cooperative downtown, where she worked three days a week. She managed to eke out a living. The accident had set her back.

"Wouldn't you know it, my car got stolen about ten days ago, which I'd just got back from the shop. Some kids joyriding. They hot-wired it," she said, a new word for her vocabulary. "Only they ran it into a tree—didn't hurt anyone fortunately. Only it's back in the shop."

"Kids are wild these days," he sympathized. "No discipline. It's the parents' fault."

It was also youth, she wanted to tell him, the giddiness and wildness and sheer force of it. "It'll take us a while to get straightened out," she said as she followed him out the door and into the yard, trying to mollify him for the circumstances she found herself in. She hated it when she got pushed into the arena of officialdom. They walked round to the back, a tangle of weeds. He flicked through a notebook and extracted an envelope. "The city has given you thirty days." He paused to

48

look at a path of mole mounds, small volcanoes. Life under the surface. Then he tripped into a hole Lavinia's dog, Siegfried, had created in search of a bone that was no doubt somewhere else. He had a poor memory for bones no interest in moles.

She caught at the fellow's arm as he flailed to regain his balance. "It's all right," he insisted. "Good thing I didn't break a leg."

She agreed wholeheartedly.

"Are there snakes in that grass? The neighbor thought there were snakes."

And who could that have been? she wondered. The Jacksons on one side, the Filmores on the other? The people in back with the huge van? Someone across the street? "If there are," she said, "they've got a job to do on those moles."

He consulted his notebook again. "That would make it September 25th," he said. "You have till then. Have a good weekend," he said.

"You think that hurricane's going to hit New Orleans?" she said—it was on her mind.

'I'm glad it's not me down there," he said, before he turned away.

She contemplated the porch for a moment before she went inside. "Well, Jade, here it all is—what you've collected." She could hardly see into the pile to know what was there. The table with legs that needed gluing. The bureau that would bring big bucks once Jade found a marble top to replace the one missing and found new drawer handles. And the old trunk with flowers stamped into tin sidepanels and on the top that somebody in the throes of nostalgia was bound to shell out for. Ditto for the old wheelbarrow. Must be over a hundred years old. The magic words. Destined to confer value. Broken tables, bottomless chairs—all that was stained, warped, disdained would be transformed into collectibles along with a new life for Jade, who once and for all would leave behind the trail of frustrated efforts and failures: colleges dropped out of, jobs abandoned, boyfriends sent packing, various projects come to grief, bills unpaid, two cats left to fend

49

for themselves. All in the high winds of desperation.

Maggie had to be careful not to put any doubts in the way, encouraging Jade till the flame flickered and caught, soothing her past discouragements; already there seemed a mountain to move.

There was activity on the front porch. The trunk with the stamped flowers had worked its appeal on Jade. She'd had a vision of what it could be and had bolted downtown for some acrylic paints. She was now painting all the flowers. Painstaking work. The rest of the trunk she had painted blue. Maggie stopped to admire it on her way to pick up her car from the shop. "Looking good," she said. And how much, she wondered, could Jade possibly charge to make up for the hours of her labor?

"You really like it?" Jade said. She stood up and eyed her work critically.

"I think it's splendid," Maggie said. No doubt about it. Jade's instinct for beauty was beyond reproach.

Inside, Lavinia was getting ready to entertain. Every Thursday, Myra Spears, a musician who sold Avon products, came for tea. That she had played the flute for a small ensemble put her well above the rest of their acquaintances. Lavinia would be put in mind of things she loved, while Myra sat spellbound listening to her reminisce.

"You've had such an exciting life," she would say deferentially. "And such talent." Lavinia had played her one of her recordings. "Just look at me now." Together they would bemoan her condition.

She had been part of the household for the past several years. Maggie had taken her in, her older sister, because she had nowhere to go. Her life, full of drama, had unrolled like one of the operas she'd starred in till her voice, as well as her manager, had betrayed her. He'd absconded with all her money, leaving her in shock, stripped of all she'd been accustomed to. Even though reduced to penury, she could never forget she was a diva who had sung in the major opera houses of Europe. Maggie's problems with the city and Jade's efforts on the porch were as far from her consciousness as the impending hurricane.

When Maggie stepped outdoors, choosing to walk the three miles to the garage, the sky was clear. Still summery, a light breeze playing through the maples. For a moment she felt almost happy. After she'd driven her car off the lot, she stopped by the employment office to see if she could find a couple of men who could tackle the yard and help clear the porch. They could use Jade's truck to cart off the dead branches that had fallen from the trees. But she found only a couple of sad-looking women, one with a small girl, filing for unemployment compensation and an older man who was looking for a night clerk's job.

But her luck took a sudden shift as she was nearing home. Just down the street she spotted a man mowing the lawn, a yellow truck parked at the curb whose side was painted with palm trees and birds of paradise. Letters formed of leaves and flowers spelled out the name *Dominique Desjardins: For your house and yard the gift of beauty*. And it was perhaps Dominique himself out in front doing the ordinary work of cutting grass-lithe and loose-limbed. His head, surrounded by a crown of curly dark hair, gave him the appearance of some wild bloom himself. His tawny skin caught the light.

She parked her Chevy, stepped out, and waved to him as he approached behind his mower. He shut off the motor, stood up, and gave her a smile and nod, followed by a little sweep of the hand as though she were an invited guest.

"Listen—" she said. No use beating around the bush. Either he'd do it or he wouldn't. "I've got a mess up at my place. Weeds like you wouldn't believe. Branches down all over the yard. Furniture piled up on the porch. The city's on my tail to get things cleaned up. And my money's just about . . ."

He held up his hand. "Oh, no hurry, ma'am," he said. "You fire like a machine gun. Just take your time." His voice caressed the words as though each sound was a gift to the ear. Not quite a song, but enough to carry her into a different rhythm. The man himself seemed not quite real, the way the sun played on his face and was given back in subtle lights. He stood at ease; he had all the time in the world. Or else he had shed time, just passed right through it. No wonder he had interrupted her. Suddenly over-whelmed, she could hardly speak. She wanted to lean her head against his chest and weep.

"I don't know what sort of work you do," she said in a low voice.

"I do all kind of things," he said, with a soft laugh and ges-tured toward the side of the truck. "I mow lawns and pull weeds and plant grass and flowers. And what's broken I can fix."

How about my life? she wanted to say. Just for starters. She was staring at the side of the truck, taking in something she had missed before. Or had it actually been there? *Spirit work*, she read.

"You mean my sign," he said, and laughed again, as at a joke they both shared. "If spirit don't help, it all comes to nothing. The yard don't prosper and the house ain't fit for living."

"You got it," she said, and stood dumbfounded. Here was the impasse that had confronted her.

He gave her a little pat on the shoulder. "Just tell me what you need—tell me slow."

She described the yard and reeled off what had to be done. She didn't ask the price. Like time, it didn't seem part of the consideration. Here was the man to help her, if anyone could.

"Why don't I just swing by when I get done here," he said. "I never know what the job requires till I plant myself right in the middle."

Encouraged, she wrote down her address and drove home to wait for him.

An hour or so later his truck pulled up in front and he emerged. Jade was still working on the trunk when he arrived. "Hey, that's real nice," he said, pausing to look at Jade's flowers, as Maggie stepped out to meet him. "Looks like you got a heap of stuff here to do," he said.

Jade looked at him. "Looks like it," she said dryly.

"I'll show you what has to be done in the yard," Maggie said. "Jade's cut the grass in front, but the back yard's gotten out of hand. I've been laid up."

"Things can get away from you," he sympathized. He looked up and around. "Sun's good today," he said, extending his palms, feeling out the light. "Hot and lovely—good for flower beds once we get those weeds cleared out. You got some nice shade trees here."

Only they would shed their leaves again where she had let the others lie till they rotted into the ground. Good for the soil anyway—and the weeds. He followed her around the yard, where the grasshoppers, at their approach, shot up and out in all directions. "All this," she indicated.

"I see you got an apple tree over there. A couple of cherries."

"Just a few small wormy apples," she said. "The birds get the cherries."

"Needs some pruning and a little juice," he said. "Same for that lilac. Get rid of all those old canes and she'll bloom. You got irises—a sweet flower if ever there was one. Clean out those beds and separate those rhizomes, and you'll see a difference." He made slow turns about the yard, Maggie following, being shown now here, now there, plants she had forgotten. Had let go of . . . So many things, it seemed. Slipping away into time.

"We can have it all in shape," he said. "I can see this place shooting out like fireworks. Flowers everywhere. Just takes a little doing."

Even as he lifted her into the cadence of his speech, the yard seemed to blossom around her. But she dared not let him seduce her with false hope.

"My daughter collected all that furniture on the porch," she explained. "Trying to start her own business. Only . . ."

"Well," Dominique said, "things slow down for me in another month. If she wants some help with the repairing and refinishing . . ."

"I think that would be terrific," Maggie said. They went back to the porch. Jade had gone somewhere meanwhile, leaving her paints and brushes. Her truck was gone as well. "I hope the two of you can work something out." Dominique went over to a bureau, pulled out the drawers, examined the interior, flipped away a loose scab of paint with a fingernail. "Some good wood here," he said.

"She has an eye for things. A way of imagining. Can see the possibility in them."

"That's a gift," Dominique said. "What keeps me going. Whenever I get in a tight spot, I picture gardens. Then I go round smelling the flowers just like they were there." He laughed.

A tropical mentality—she envied it.

"I tell you what—if she's willing. Every time I'm close I'll run by and take whatever I've got room for. I got a dolly I can bring. Just take it back to the shop and see what I can do. Maybe we can make a deal."

When he left, Maggie felt a rising excitement. Something new had entered the equation, and she allowed herself room to imagine beyond the present. Things could change? Was that too absurd a notion?

That Saturday, Jade had gone to an estate sale out in the country. She returned followed by two men she'd hired to bring home her latest prize. It was an awkward and obviously heavy piece not to be left on the front porch, where it might attract the wrong sort of attention. She held the screen as they maneuvered it in. "There," Jade directed them. "In front of the couch." Marigold, the orange striped cat, who'd been occupying a corner of it, left off washing a paw, leapt down, and fled into the kitchen, where Maggie was cooking a chicken for supper. "Jade, is that you? What's all the commotion?"

"Come see," Jade said. Maggie emerged in time to see her counting out bills to two well-muscled young men. "Thanks, fellas," she said.

"Hope you enjoy the table," the stockier of the two said, with what Maggie thought was a hint of irony.

"What is this?"

"Look, can't you see? It's a coffin. Look at that wood. Pine, but it's aged and see the grain—wonderful color. Must be a hundred years old. And they've made it into a table. A coffin table. Isn't that wild?"

Maggie, stunned by visual proof that you could make a table out of anything, said, "What are you going to do with it?"

"Sell it, of course. Think of what it'll bring. Fortunately the dealers weren't pushing up the prices at this sale. Rather a small affair. Otherwise I could never have gotten it. It's been out in the barn for God knows how long."

A coffin in the living room. What was she supposed to do about this reorientation of space and mind? Coffin transformed into living room furniture—awaiting your teacup or wineglass. You'd have to protect the surface with coasters like any other. Yes, the pine, though rough, held some interest. To a great degree she shared Jade's passion for wood. Before she could determine how to take in this change of perspective, Lavinia appeared.

She'd just come in from a walk with her ancient poodle, and was stopped in her tracks. "What is this?" she demanded. "It looks like . . ."

"It is," Jade assured her. "A coffin. A pine coffin. They weren't so tall in those days, so it's not a big one. Must have been a leftover. Somebody made it into a table."

"You're not going to bring that thing in here?"

Maggie was frowning, waving a hand, trying to fend her off.

But Lavinia ignored her. "We *live* here—didn't that occur to you? That is, we're *trying* to live here."

"It's temporary," Jade said. "Till I can sell it. You don't have to look at it."

"Are you mad? You think you can be in this room without knowing it's there?"

Jade shrugged. "It's my business—my way of earning a living. The shed's full."

"But perhaps we can make some space," Maggie suggested. "Move a few things around. It might not sell immediately . . ."

"You think you can do anything." Lavinia had been set in motion, and now she was carried forward by the momentum of a rage that was never fully banked—"You think you're always entitled. Look at your mother—just look at her. Doesn't have a mind of her own anymore. You say 'Jump,' and she jumps."

"Oh, go sing in the church choir," Jade said, ready to take her on. "A bunch of yellow newspaper clippings—that's all you are."

"Both of you . . ."

"No," Lavinia said, drawing herself up. "That's not what I am. I had a talent, and I used it. I struggled and let it enter the world. Nobody can take that from me. What have you brought into this house but junk that ought to be thrown away?"

"And you still act like you're queen of the hive. Everybody has to cater to you, walk around on eggshells because you're the great Lena Mock. Pardon me—Lavinia Tucker, transformed by celebrity. Who even remembers your name? Who comes to see you? You'd starve if . . ."

"Stop it!" Maggie yelled. "Both of you.

"I won't live with that thing in this house," Lavinia raged. "Throw me out in the street if you want to." Siegfried, dancing around among them, paused to piddle on the floor. Lavinia turned and fled to her room.

"The bitch," Jade said. "Please," Maggie said.

"The way you cater to her," Jade said. "Taking her around to all the department stores to look at stuff she can't buy. So she can go to the dollar store and pick up a box of fake fancy crackers and a jar of cheese to entertain the Avon lady. The Avon lady, for God's sake. To impress her. And those costumes she brings out—grand wardrobe. That ragged fox-fur piece. She's got the same kind of little beady eyes. Disgusting."

"It's her only happiness," Maggie said. "She was Carmen; she was Desdemona. She had bouquets thrown at her feet . . ."

"Let her eat them." She turned away. "Why is she entitled to everything when I'm only trying . . ." Helplessly, Maggie held out her arms, took her in, smoothed her back, tried to reassure her. Jade pulled away. "You don't even know me," she said.

Now they were both looking at the aftermath, as though trying to assess the damage after a windshear. Jade had packed up in the middle of the night, having rifled the little lacquered box with the lions painted on it where Maggie kept the household money, and left the two women for the golden sheen of a future yet to be discovered. How often had it happened?

They stood looking past the open door of Jade's room, surveying a chaos beyond the typical mess she'd always lived in—drawers pulled open, clothes lying helter-skelter. Maggie picked up a necklace she'd given Jade for her birthday a month earlier and surveyed a shelf with various books, pictures, and keepsakes. When Jade packed up and moved on, the sheer force of motive thrust her past all possessions and distractions.

"I'll say only what I've said long ago," Lavinia insisted. "She's abused you and you've let her. Always ready to lay yourself on the altar of sacrifice-believe everything she says, go along with whatever cockamamie scheme she comes up with, but I knew in my heart of hearts.' The recitative. The tone gathering in the tragic irony, but with a hint of triumph, as Maggie kept to her silence, wiping her eyes.

Lavinia's talent had been noticed early, given full attention and all the family resources. Maggie's gift, conferred perhaps by the thirteenth fairy, had been the gift of uncertainty, a continual struggle to become anything at all. Then, getting pregnant just out of high school, she had become a mother. Jade was her child in more ways than one.

Now among Lavinia's advantages was that she had at least the language of the stage to call upon. Large gestures, emphatic syllables. "I could see it coming." She could have launched into the aria, "I told you so," in the mezzo-soprano range, hitting the high notes of the resentment she felt toward Jade, who kept throwing away her chances, when her own had been reduced to nil and she'd been left to depend on Maggie's charity.

Wind and water. Destruction and chaos. The ruin of New Orleans. Maggie had watched the nightmare unfold on television and in the newspaper. People crammed into the Super Dome, where the forces of nature had taken over as well. Rape, murder, pillage, police brutality. She was haunted by the voices of those who'd lost the last vestige of shelter and the little treasures of their lives; by the faces of relatives searching for sisters and mothers, fathers and children, abandoned pets; by the images of dead bodies and alligators and dogs and cats floating in what had been streets.

Moved to create some sort of order, she spent the morning in Jade's room putting things away. For a moment she was standing inside Jade herself following the urge for beauty that expressed itself in the prints on her walls, the rocks she collected, the little designs she made for stationery and bookmarks. Her childhood had been a passion of making things.

Afterward she went to the grocery. They would have food on the table, water to drink. They still had a roof over their heads. That much at least—it was a great deal. That afternoon Dominique was supposed to come by. On her return she found Lavinia and Myra having tea at the dining-room table. Their Thursday tete-a-tete. There'd been a sale on Earl Grey, Maggie remembered. And the cookies, too, had been marked down. They were sitting with their backs to the living room, and apparently they hadn't heard Maggie enter.

"What I have suffered at her hands," Lavinia was saying. "Crazy, that's all you can say. You've seen that awful thing in the living room."

Maggie threw her packages onto the living-room couch, and the two women looked up, startled.

"We didn't hear you come in," Lavinia said.

"I came on ghost feet," Maggie said. She was still standing in the living room, taking off her sun hat. No one used the living room any longer except as a passageway to somewhere else. Even the animals avoided it. Once Lavinia came to the piano to practice scales, first putting an afghan over the coffin-table. She tried one of her favorite arias till her voice went off key, and she shut the instrument with an impatient flourish. "It's the atmosphere in here," she complained. "That awful table exerts its influence even under cover. My voice has been like this ever since it entered the house."

Maggie, too, avoided the living room; it brought back the whole anguish of Jade's sojourn in the house, its fruitless conclusion, and the long history of abortive efforts that had gone before. In the evenings after supper she drank her tea and read in the kitchen, where the light seemed friendlier. There had been no word from Jade

"Dominique's coming by," Maggie told Lavinia after Myra had left. "He's going to do some work in the yard."

"Well, the first thing he'd better do is take that table," Lavinia said. "I can't sleep with that thing in the house. It twists my dreams out of shape."

The world does that too, Maggie thought.

"I tell you, the thing scares me. This house . . . what will become of us—I think about it constantly."

"Don't remind me," Maggie said softly.

When Dominique arrived, she had him come into the house before he started work. "My daughter's gone," she said in a low voice. "Just took off," she said. "It's not the first time. I can't tell you how often I've tried. All kinds of things to get her on the right track. And always it turns wrong." Her hands went to her face. She couldn't stop talking. "If only I'd . . ."

"It was nothing you done," he said, putting his hands on her shoulders. "Nothing you done or didn't do. Maybe it's like she's got a cocoon wrapped around her and she's living inside, and the inside is different from the outside. Like a story she's done told herself and got to keep telling herself."

Is that how it is? she wondered. And do you ever break out? She brought herself back to purpose. "Now I have to do something with all the stuff out there. This is the last thing she bought," Maggie said, leading him past the cat-clawed armchair to the table.

"And it's the one thing I wish you'd take first," Lavinia said, emerging from the kitchen. "Supposed to be a coffee table," she said. "A coffin table. Great joke, isn't it?"

"Ever opened it?" Dominique said. The three of them stood gazing down at it.

"Heavens, no."

"Bet there's a spirit inside just waiting to get out."

"I thought spirits could walk through walls," Maggie said. "Depends on the spirit. Some just get trapped and stay in one spot for years and centuries. Till somebody comes along and sets them free."

"Well, for my money, it can stay put," Lavinia said and left them to walk her dog.

"Yeah," he said to Maggie. "You never know what you might be in for." He shifted from one foot to the other. "Only I have to bring Jimmy around to help me with it. Next time I'm around."

"I just want you to take it away," she said, with a desperation that surprised her.

After he left, she felt unsettled, jumpy. A new breach had appeared in the state of her affairs with a chill wind ripping through it. The coffin table seemed to fill the house and consume her thought. Now her imagination was full of what might be in it, the unseen hazards she might be living with. The dead in the living room. Having it there one more day, one more hour . . . She felt again a passion that seemed peculiarly hers–a terrible longing that things might change.

She couldn't sleep. She woke up in the still hours to what she thought was the sound of groaning and got up and turned on all the lights. She tiptoed into the living room, where, except for the boards that creaked underfoot and the crepitations in the walls, all was as she'd left it. Perhaps Siegfried had had a bad dream. Suppose something was indeed trapped inside. Suppose she did lift the lid. It would take courage. And she wasn't strong enough. Weak and witless. When she went back to bed, she lay in the dark and once again thought she heard a sound—of moaning or mourning. She put a pillow over her head.

When Dominique appeared, with his helper in tow, Maggie could have thrown her arms around him. But as he stood in front of the table, he shook his head. "Can't take it away yet," he said. "Spirit don't like it."

She felt condemned. "Didn't we submit the proper forms?" she asked. "Do we need a special password?" She had never claimed ownership. It was there only because of Jade. It didn't belong to her, and she had no wish to claim it. Now it appeared a spirit was in charge and she was somehow responsible. Dominique gave a little shrug. "Sometimes waiting's the best. See what it wants."

"Seems like I've waited all my life." She wanted to turn away from the day. But at least he and Jimmy did take action in the backyard, cutting down dead limbs, collecting fallen branches and chopping them up till they all formed a neat stack-wood for the fireplace. Then the two men started digging up plants and reviving an old circle with bricks around it to replant them. They went over the yard with a rototiller and raked over the surface. That afternoon he came round to put in grass. He got a start on the other beds, cutting down saplings and clearing away vines. She could decide what she wanted to plant. He ended up by taking one of the bureaus and a table from the front porch in exchange for the work. The porch displayed a small cleared area.

The coffin table remained where it was.

He came round the next morning so early she was still in her robe.

"Sorry to disturb you," he said, "but I got to take off."

"Take off? Why are you leaving Metairie? Where are you go-ing?"

"New Orleans," he said. "I got to go back."

"Oh, but you can't leave," she protested.

"I got to go," he said. "I promised Sister Gertrude I'd be there if she ever needed help, and she's calling me back. I can hear her voice inside me."

"Oh," she said, devastated.

"Can't refuse," he said. "She's the one give me everything made me what I am. She was a terror all right." He smiled over the memory. "Said to me, 'Brother, you going come to your death in the gutter. And nobody to fetch you out. The bottle or the needle—that what you want?'"

"Taught me planting—yeah, she's the one. Give me my name. Dominique." He smiled. "Garden Master. Instead of Tommy in the Ditch."

"When will you be back?" she ventured.

"Can't say for sure."

"Oh." *Maybe never—she* sank with the idea.

After Dominique left she walked around the yard, trying to look at what had been done—staring blankly. Bleakly. Abandoned there with everything yet to do.

In the house the coffin table waited. Was there some sort of emanation that coalesced in all their troubled dreams and rose up like a miasma that moved even beyond the house? And what would clear it away? Something like the hurricane—ripping ev-erything apart, bringing all to light: the hidden corruption re-vealed, the rickety structures built on the generations of pover-ty and neglect and entrapment? Everything swept upside down, turned inside out. Houses becoming coffins as the water rose in the living rooms up to the bedrooms, sending people to attics and roofs, where so many waited in vain. The stored-up agony throwing itself outward on the flood. Wind and water sweeping through, leaving behind the debris.

"Seems I'm stuck with you," she said. She could almost see something there inside, not just trapped—but struggling to get out. Herself? Jade? Both of them? Even Lavinia? But maybe something larger yet that took them in, the embodiment of strug gle itself. Waiting to get out. She could feel its yearning as it joined her own.

It all had to come out—to be seen, everything in the light. It was there pushing forward, telling her what she had to do. Create something, as she'd always had to do, but this time with greater devotion, once again seizing upon the imperatives of the imagination as each moment required. And she could see herself in an emboldened moment opening the lid. Opening it up, letting out what?—oh, yes, herself—and rising, oh, yes, rising till she was there over the water—rising with whatever it was as it moved out over the water, over the troubled streets and the broken lives, facing the void-for what could she know with surety?—looking and searching, yes, until she could find Dominique dreaming of gardens.

THE ORANGE BIRD

The crate from Spain, long awaited, arrived at the gallery that morning. Mildred was all agog, a kid getting a birthday present, hovering over Mark as he cut the wires and pried up the planks. Carl and Antonia stood by, witnesses of the grand opening. She'd been on pins and needles for months—would the shipment arrive, would Diego come through? This was her baby. She winced as the nails came out, as though Mark might damage something, and it would be hell to pay if he did. He worked loose the lid, took out the packing. A blast of color struck him in the eye. Careful of the baby, he lifted the top canvas and set it up on a chair. The four of them stood back appraising. There it was: a vase of red and yellow flowers like fried eggs, a drape to one side; in the background an amorphous mauve shape next to what could have been a corner of the Alhambra. In front, a lobster, cooked and coral. On the other side a basket with clusters of grapes spilling out, two apples in the neighborhood, an orange bird behind. As a finishing touch the surface offered a crackled effect. Breathtakingly awful.

"It's beyond imagination," Mildred enthused. "Just look at the color."

Mark caught Antonia's eye, but her expression was neutral. "You can certainly see the Spanish touch," she said. He covered his mouth to avoid some expression of horror, to still the laughter that threatened to double him over. Mildred shot him a glance, dismissed him. If she'd caught his disloyalty, it didn't matter.

"Well, Diego's really done me proud," Mildred said, turning the paintings over to Carl, who did most of the framing. Eleven more lay in the crate, looking as though they'd been cranked out by a machine. "A black frame," Carl said, "to lock in the color. Or maybe silver." Carl, expert at measuring and cutting, never had an opinion about anything he was asked to frame. Just so there were no complaints from the customer. Antonia was a different kettle of fish.

"I'm just thrilled," Mildred said. "It's so hard to get a still life that'll go over. People get bored with the same old stuff. I've seen too many pumpkins in my time. I've got to call the Steens." She went off to do so at once.

Thrilled. To have hit upon Spanish kitsch instead of the mere domestic species. No doubt offering employment to how many struggling, or maybe not so struggling, Spanish artists. "Thrilled? She can't believe that's art," Mark said to Antonia after Mildred had left for the bank. "It belongs in WalMart."

"Does it matter?" She was a small energetic woman in her fif ties, a photographer who supplemented her income by working part-time in the gallery and by doing weddings. She liked the connection. She and Mildred had been on friendly terms for years. A few prints of her photographs, studies in light and shad- ow, offering haunting contrasts, hung on the walls, attracting an occasional buyer. To Mark, these were the best work in the gal- lery. "Believe me, Mildred knows what she's doing. She's had to learn the hard way."

He tried for a title. "'The Afternoon of the Lobster Qua drille"—how does that grab you?"

It's apretty inert lobster."

"A more Daliesque approach? 'The Cornucopia's Lament'? 'Sancho Panza Strikes Again' or 'The Persistence of Indigestion'?"

"You haven't quite caught the essence. It has a certain ge- nius," Antonia said, cocking her head, as though to capture it more fully. "A genius of badness—that's hard to come by."

"I think Mildred's outdone herself."

Transcending the typical, the banal, the decorative, this was their bread and butter. Landscapes of houses and trees decked in summer green; seascapes with foam, and sometimes dramatic clouds; the snows of a New England winter—the "yesteryear stuff," he called it—what would go well in a dining room or over the mantel of a fireplace. Technical skill to the grommet. ("Don't knock it," Antonia said. "Considering the way they come out of some of the art schools these days. Can't draw for shit."—"I don't," he insisted.) Still anybody could have painted them. No character, no signature. Early Motel. Late Professional Building. For the suburban nests of the up and grasping, fine for bank or doctor's office. It didn't offend anyone—maybe even convinced people there was a place for art. For artists. For himself—or so he hoped.

He figured he'd hit it lucky when Mildred took him on his first year out of art school. Except for the few who'd landed on their feet, who'd somehow gotten connections and were consistently selling their work, most of his buddies had either gone into advertising or into some form of computer graphics. A wonderfully talented watercolorist was taken on by a greeting-card company. Left to his own devices, he'd managed to cobble together various part-time jobs. For a time he worked nights in a bakery, after which he threw himself exhausted into bed. Then the gallery job opened up, offering him a glimpse into the art scene and actually allow ing him time to paint on his own. For the moment, at least, he felt he was struggling in the right direction. If most of the stuff Mildred sold was nothing he'd ever paint himself, at least he didn't have to think about it. His work there was varied enough to be interesting: talking to potential buyers, trying to connect them with what they were looking for, whatever it was, or else setting up the shows. These were often the work of artists who combined fabric-and-Hower arrangements, did playful treatments of animals, or water colors of river, lake, and rocky abutment. Occasionally Mildred took in a painter who moved in the direction of abstraction or did something unusual with color. Mark had hung a couple of shows that moved toward the pretty good.

So far the only work that genuinely interested him was Antonia's photographs. When he tried to tell her how good they were, her face reddened, as though he'd discovered a secret that couldn't bring her any benefit. "I'm very grateful to Mildred," she'd say, as though her talent was owing to her as well. "She actually has one hanging in her living room."

Her first years Mildred had taken up young and promising artists and given them shows, even though their work mostly didn't sell, and more than once she'd been left in the lurch. She hadn't done that for quite a while, but had subsided into success. She had, in fact, hit the jackpot several years back when she'd been the one to handle the contract for the paintings and assorted art objects for a cluster of condomin iums going up. Some artists both in the area and outside had been commissioned to do paintings, even a few sculptures, suitable not only for living and dining rooms, but for bedrooms and hallways. Mildred had made it into a real competition, had worked up a lot of publicity in the papers. Artists had submitted slides for the project, and Mildred had made the selections. They'd filled up the place with beach scenes at sunrise and sunset, flower arrangements, birds in flight. Pinks and peaches, vibrant greens and blues and lavenders going from sultry to misty. The impression apparently was to make the midwestern city-dweller believe he'd been transported to Florida. "Mildred made a bundle," Antonia had told him. "Really expanded her collection. You should see that place of hers."

By all descriptions a real showplace. Expensive woods, stone fireplace. One of the best private art collections she'd seen in the city. Not just prints and ceramics by Matisse and Picasso— the Names—but lithographs by Romare Bearden, paintings by Wayne Thiebaud, Alice Neel, Chuck Close, and other notables. Work that took not just money-apparently she had plenty to throw around—but an eye too.

Mildred was a puzzle to him. Her little-kid excitement over the hopelessly bad seesawing with her aim to live with the good stuff. For investment purposes? To show she had class? She knew how to make a buck—you had to give her that. But beyond that? He wanted a way past equivocation, to where their sympathies might join—especially when she said just before the shipment arrived, "Hey, what are you painting these days? I'd like to see your work."

He was flattered, yet reluctant, at the same time curious to see what her response might be. Actually he felt pretty good about what he was doing. He hadn't found an approach that satisfied him; he was still trying to break loose from the school stuff he'd done, most-ly abstract expressionist displays with heavy impasto and a lot of surging shapes, work that now struck him as turgid and derivative, whatever praise he might have received. Now he was working into a more figurative mode, trying to use color with more finesse. Af-ter a long love affair with the German expressionists, Mark realized Bonnard had become his idol.

Then she mentioned it again. "When are you going to bring something in?" When he did, taking in half a dozen of his recent canvases, Mildred set them up along the wall, regarded them with a critical eye. "You're working out of the dead stuff," she told him. "That's good." Hardly the enthusiasm that met the Spanish still life, but better than nothing. "Keep moving. Bring some more when you get them done."

He couldn't help an occasional fantasy—her giving him a show, inviting him to her house to see her art work . . . All very unlikely, he told himself.

"Twelve of them," he said to Antonia. "How in the hell can she sell twelve of *those?* Impossible."

"You want to bet on it?" Antonia said, giving a little ironic smile.

"Okay," he said. "You win, I'll buy you a beer at Stefanelli's."
"If I lose."

"I'll buy you a beer anyway." If he could manage it. Right now he was pressed from all sides—student loans, a car going bad, a nagging weakness in the chest he hadn't yet taken to a doctor.

She laughed. "You're on. Only if you win . . ."

"Trade me one of your photographs for one of my paintings."

"A deal. You look like you could use some coffee. I'll make some." She moved toward the back.

"Thought it was my turn."

"You can do it next time."

He was bone tired. He'd stayed up most of the night working on a painting that refused to jell. Tonight he'd take a break, head off to Stefanelli's and sit around with the old Italian men still in the neighborhood who frequented the place. For some reason he felt more at home with them than with the young guys that hung around. They were no longer trying to prove anything—a relief. Especially if you had everything to prove yourself. It was his only social life, as much as he could afford. As it was, he made barely enough to pay the rent on an apartment in a rundown blue-collar neighborhood, the living room serving as his studio. He'd rigged up a set of lights so he could work nights after he got home. Usually Mark managed a couple or three hours of painting, but sometimes when he really got going, he stayed up till all hours. He dared not do it often—he couldn't risk falling asleep on the job. He lived for his two days off, Sunday and Monday, when he could work uninterruptedly, sleeping late and working all day. He'd lost touch with most of his college friends. When one of them called, he was eager enough to talk on the phone but was vague about future meetings—at least for the time being. To all intents and purposes he'd gone into hibernation. He had work to do, had to see what was in him.

The first of the Spanish still lifes sold the next week. It was just what the Steens wanted. He drew a quick sketch of them in the little book he carried in his pocket: a large, hearty woman with graying hair, who wore huge earrings with smiley faces, and her balding mate, who spoke in quick explosive bursts: "Terrific color—light up that north wall come winter, won't it, hon? Terrific color."

"I was sure you'd like it," Mildred said.

Antonia gave him a significant look. Okay, one down. Mildred hung up a second and sold it the same week, this time to a woman who came in with a handsome full-size poodle.

The sketches became a series, expanding like a rogues' gallery. As a preface he'd written, *What do these faces have in common?*

After the eleventh had sold, in less than three months, Mark conceded that he owed Antonia a beer. That is, if he could afford it. He'd just gotten his car out of the shop, the eighteen-year-old TransAm he'd taken over from his uncle. Twelve hundred bucks on his credit card, not to mention the interest. The zeros on the bill haunted him. More out of desperation than hope, he decided to ask Mildred if she'd give him a show. His work was taking shape; it had some flashes here and there. If he could sell a few paintings . . . make a small debut. He went back over her responses as though he were counting credits. "Nice color going there." "The shapes in that one—very organic." Had anything impressed her?

He approached her at her desk cluttered with catalogs and brochures, the last Spanish still life emphatically occupying the wall just behind. She looked up from a catalog she was examining.

"An exhibit?" he asked.

"Old friend of mine from school," she said. He drew up to look over her shoulder, while she turned the pages. Mountains, cactus-studded landscapes, horses. Portraits of Hispanics. Nothing new, but genuinely well done. "She's got something," he said, leaning forward to read the name. Heather Duncan.

"A lot of talent. She used to do things like you'd see in a dream. I've got one in my bedroom. Went out to Santa Fe a few years back. Now they're selling everything she paints. Yeah," she said. "She's finally done it."

"Some great artists have gone out there to New Mexico. Such a powerful landscape."

She didn't seem to hear him. "All she needs are a few cows' skulls."

"You going out for the opening?" he said, feeling some idiotic need to put off what he wanted to ask her.

"Too many things pressing," she said.

Then she said, "Sit down. There's something I've been thinking about. I just wanted to be sure it was the right moment."

His heart took a sudden leap, even as the Spanish still life met his eye and the orange bird seemed to stare right through him.

"Can you paint one of these?" she asked him, gesturing toward the painting.

You've got to be kidding, he almost blurted out. He was struck dumb. "Nobody's ever asked me," he said.

"I'm offering you a chance," she said. "There are lots of young artists around who could use the money."

Including himself. "Well, I . . ."

"Of course you can," she said, suddenly beaming at him. "I know you can—I've seen your work. Two hundred apiece," she said; "plus," she added indulgently, "an allowance for canvases and paints. I want another twelve of them."

Enough to get himself out of hock and have a little to float on. Would it be selling his soul? But then maybe he could actually learn something, improve some of his techniques. Like the apprentices in the old days. The idea was beginning to appeal to him. "I'll give it a whirl," he said.

"Good boy," she said. "I knew you had it in you."

He spent the next Sunday stretching and gessoing canvases. He'd brought home the still life and hung it up on the wall, where, with the lights on it, it gave off an unholy garish sheen. He planted himself in front of it and tried to figure out the colors. Mix and match. When in doubt, lay on the cadmiums. Orange, red, yellow. After his initial drawing and painting classes, his struggling beginner's efforts, he hadn't done any close copying. But he figured he'd go about it the way he'd seen it done in the textbooks: make a grid, block out the forms, sketch in the details, set up some good background colors. Since this was a production job, he could try laying in the larger areas, moving from one canvas to another. He did the drape, the slab of building, the ambiguous mauve shape, then back to the first, working toward the more challenging objects. The flowers he found monstrously difficult—gaudy, truculent, but somehow elusive, innocent even in their vulgarity. He thought of Mildred. He had to keep the colors clean, pay attention to the parts but not neglect the whole. In its way, it all had to work—flowers, basket, grapes, apples, lobster, bird. As Antonia suggested, there was a certain

71

genius in it. You had to find your way into that, on the terms it demanded. Harder than he thought—more time-consuming than he expected. For when he got through the first, the painting stood inert before his eyes. Still life *indeed-nature morte*. So what was wrong?

Every night he came home from work and after a quick supper—a sandwich, a can of soup heated up, or a frozen pizza he popped into the oven—he approached the painting with a certain dread, while the rest stood lined up against the wall. For two or three hours he tried to meet it on his own terms. He had to wipe away any trace of a smirk, humble himself; otherwise it wouldn't yield. Sometimes he wanted to weep with vexation—the damned thing wasn't worth the effort. Then one night when he'd almost despaired, it all came together. Just like that, as though something had sneaked in when he wasn't looking. He worked in a frenzy till four in the morning. Then it was finished, sweet Jesus—it was done. He collapsed into bed but couldn't sleep, fueled awake by a curious excitement, even triumph. When he finally awoke from an exhausted sleep, he had to go immediately to look at the painting. It held, cohered, made a world, out of which the orange bird met his eye with a certain fierce partiality, seemed to follow him around the room, as though he'd some how claimed it. He couldn't bear its gaze.

"Perfect," Mildred said, when he took it in. "Absolutely perfect. Look at this, will you," she said, calling over Antonia.

"I think you've even improved on it. Those flowers have a certain subtlety." She considered. "Maybe with the rest you could give the bird just a few more touches." He didn't know whether to laugh or weep.

The subsequent paintings went more quickly. Mildred thought it best that he work from his own copy rather than the original. Let there be a few distinctive touches, so long as the painting had the same impact. He was learning quickly, discovering something from each one. Now that he'd got the colors down, he began to work up a kind of shorthand, laying in some of the areas almost without thinking. He'd got the flowers under control; the grapes had taken on a kind of fullness, as though they might explode into flavor on the palate. The apples, too, more and more appealing, were al most seductive. Now it was the bird that gave him fits. What was it doing there in its orangeness? Was there such a creature? Or a figment of dream caught in a landscape it too found unreal?

Now he painted in his dreams as well as his waking hours, painted endlessly in a kind of Sisyphean labor, so that he was more exhausted when he woke than when he went to sleep. Sometimes he was in an undersea realm, trying to paint a lobster as it disappeared in a mass of undulating bodies and snapping claws. Sometimes he found piles of wormy apples he had to sort through to find the two he needed to paint. And many a night he spent looking for the orange bird, who continually eluded him, at times leaving behind a single glow ing feather. The bird challenged him in some uncanny way, and just when he'd given it up, it would appear for an instant, remote and formidable. On one occasion it landed on his shoulder, its voice in his ear, almost a human voice, but so gentle and caressing that it seemed more than human. When he woke, he felt he had gained something of incomparable value, though what he couldn't have said. When he looked at the painting, the bird confronted him as imperiously as ever, returning only his stare; and could it have uttered a sound, he would have expected a voice harsh as a crow's. From the finished canvas its eye followed him relentlessly around the room.

He wanted to be rid of its dismaying presence, wanted to be done with the whole ungodly mess. He worked as though under sentence, as though he'd entered a dimension where his dreams were part of the trial. Even as he brought in the canvases one by one, to Mildred's extravagant praise, he had no sense that he was emerging from his predicament. Then, when he brought in the twelfth—they had been selling almost as quickly as he could paint them—she said, "I want a dozen more."

He broke into a sweat. *It's killing me,* he wanted to protest. His mind leapt into consequences and options. She might can him—

and anything else he found had the prospect of being worse. "Let me think about it," he temporized.

"What's there to think?" she said. "You've got it down to a fine science. You don't have some foolish notion you're prostituting yourself?" She looked at him in amusement.

What could he say that she'd be willing to hear? That the job had been a stop-gap affair. That he was going stale with the repetition? That he had to give his energy to his own work. "Mildred," he said, "I've done twelve."

"So you want to bail out, eh? Sick of it—up to the gills with it, eh? Yeah, I've seen them, all the little boys and girls who want to do art. Do something *original*. Bum with a hard gem like flame—I've even given a few of them house room." She gave a little sniff. "How many go on and do anything worth pissing on? Answer me. One in a thousand, when all's said and done—maybe one in ten thousand. I know—the rest have their go at it. They paint their little canvases and write their little plays and audition for acting jobs, and scribble out their passionate prose. And you know what? I was among them. Can you feature that? I even won prizes." For a moment she seemed to dip down into some memory of herself that brought her to a shrug and a small ironic dismissal.

She looked at him sharply. "And what do you think you've got that's so special? Even if you had the talent, you haven't got the moxy to . . ."

"Wait a minute," he said, blindsided by her attack. What was eating her? "I thought you liked what I was doing."

"Do you know how many are operating at that level of talent? Dozens. And not a drop more. No, you don't have it. And if you ever do, it'll surprise the hell out of both of us."

"So who the hell are you?"

'I'm trying to do you a favor," she said. "Save you some grief. Reputations are made in New York," she said. "How many have got what it takes to hack it there? You may as well paint stilllifes. It'll get you farther than anything else you've done."

It was all he could do to keep from hitting her. Only there was no arguing, no proof to off er. Only the nagging suspicion that she might be right. "Okay," he said. "I'll just do that."

"Twelve more," she said.

The next week he was fueled by some sort of fever that turned days and nights into one continuous reel of shifting imag-es in his head-all with the intensity of the Spanish still life, but of a reality heightened beyond it. He hardly knew what he was doing. He called in sick, went to bed and slept and sweated for hours. When he woke, wrung out, thirsty beyond belief, he didn't know day from night. He went to the sink and poured water down his throat until he felt bloated and mopped his face. For a time he sat staring at his hand, as though it were a strange attachment for which he had not yet discovered the use. He felt an overwhelming urge to paint.

He seized a canvas he had primed and set it on the easel. From the wall where the model hung the orange bird hunched as though it were shivering in its feathers. He hardly glanced at it. He could have painted the whole thing from memory. He had grown into habit and laid in the colors he'd used a dozen times before. No sweat. Then as he surveyed the pulsating blobs of color on his palette, he was seized by something equivalent to the fever that had taken him before, and from that point on he painted like a man possessed.

Whatever object he shaped with his brush took on a life its form could hardly contain. From the grapes a bursting full-ness-within each a small universe exploding into being. The ap-ples rolled from their position lethal with temptation as the lob-ster moved in, straight from the sea, in its claw a wriggling frog with a human face. Beneath his hand, the drape and backdrop turned to rocks and trees, an original garden writhing with cop-ulating human and animal forms. Monkeys swung from the vines. He struggled for order amid the riot of color and movement. Be-fore he collapsed alto gether, the eye of the orange bird caught his and wouldn't release his gaze, as though they had made some sort of pact. It looked ready to take off for some other dimension.

He woke early, for the first time in days breathing easily. It took him a while to remember where he was or to collect any of the pieces of the previous days. He had no idea how long the fever had engulfed him. His head was cool, and he felt as though a sweet breeze was playing around him. He remembered he'd been painting. It was only six, he saw from his watch, of whatever day was dawning. He slipped on his clothes, stepped outside to breathe the air. Then he went back in, turned on the lights and stood in front of the painting. He couldn't believe it. Someone else had painted it, not himself at all—taking inspiration from some source that lay beyond him. *Well,* he thought. *Well.* For all its madcap flourishes, it seemed more real than anything else he'd ever painted.

When Mildred arrived at the gallery, he was ready for her. As she walked in the door, he stood naked but for a hastily devised loincloth, his hair matted and falling into his face. He held up the painting.

It required a moment for her to take him in. "What is this, some kind of joke? Look, I've got things to do. Are you out of your mind or what?"

"Number thirteen," he said. "The lucky number." He danced around the room with it. "I changed a few things." Suddenly there were monkeys everywhere, cavorting through the gallery, hanging from the fixtures, crapping on the floor, monkeys somersaulting, hanging by their tails. The orange bird had risen from immobility and was flapping around the room. He saw in the middle Mildred's face forming The Scream, best painted by Munch, the clock melting down the wall, courtesy of Dali, the chair she stood in front of suddenly grabbing her and closing around her ankles, thanks to Remedios Varo. The copulating figures tumbled through the gallery, while the red and yellow flowers grew gigantic as cabbages. "Get out, get out!" she yelled at him. Naked through the gallery he streaked, blowing her a kiss. Naked he bolted into the alley, monkeys clamoring around him.

A GARDEN AMID FIRES

The lake: a faint sheen. Summoned from the stillness by a chorus of birds. Summoned into light, and form. Then the sun stroking the surface into silk, with a touch of rose mist rising. Later in the morning a breeze kicking up. The lake, deep blue, surface ruffled, sparkling with diamonds. So Claire had known it from childhood, with every variation of cloud above it, approaching rain turning all to gray, lake and sky merging into one. Now, so it seemed, it would take the gods to separate sky and water. All had coalesced into gray, with a cry of absence at the heart. *Evan,* she wrote and paused, as though staring into a gap of consciousness. *You are part of this place. Think what we lived here.*

It was ground she'd retraced for the past two years, ever since things had broken apart: Evan as part of the family. Evan as father to her teenaged son. The picnics at Katahdin, the hikes up the trails. Their days here at the table where she now sat. It was the gift she'd had to offer him while she emerged from the dark time of her divorce to reclaim the lake, the woods, her garden, taking up the original flow of time and what love could offer: the chance to see things once again in the light of a vital passion.

The sound of hammering interrupted her. One of the cabins, long empty, was now claimed by new owners. From the other side of the woods separating her place from theirs, she could hear the pounding of nails, the whine of a saw. For several weekends and one long space of a week it had been going on. Once, when she was down by the dock, a burst of curses flew in her direction like a shower of stones—ah, open water, that great conveyor and talebearer. Whoever it was, he had his work cut out for him. When she'd cared about such things, she'd gone round to inspect the rotting foundation logs and sagging roof, to deplore the deterioration and neglect. The mice must have been having a field day.

Now there were kids—the first in several seasons at that end of the lake—appearing like some endangered species staging a comeback. Two boys, Kevin and Bradley, ten and eight, were already a presence. They kept showing up just under her kitchen window, popping out of the moment, fish ing poles over their shoulders. Until August 6th they had license to make whatever depredations they could against the trout in the nearby brook. They spent hours at it. "Hey, Mrs. Lady—" Here they were again. They'd had trout for breakfast, they told her, pausing to give her the latest news of their activities. They intended to catch enough fish for supper. See. They held up their trophies. Kevin had three fish, Bradley two. They were calling it quits for lunch—was it so late already?—but they'd be back.

No doubt. They kept claiming her attention, as though by some previously determined mandate. Kevin, she paused to observe, had sandy curly hair and freckles; dimples came with a smile meant to be winning, but it was too quick, too nervous for the desired effect—an arrow fallen short of target. A few more seasons and he'd no doubt guess where to look for victories. Bradley, a beautiful boy, she acknowledged thick dark hair and blue eyes, a spot of pink on his cheek had a hangdog look. She saw awkwardness and accident, something bred for calamity. He seemed to cling to his brother, as though it were already part of his knowledge.

Since they'd been coming these past several weekends while their parents banged and sawed away, Kevin taking charge, Bradley struggling to keep up, the two of them had been on the heels of everything that moved in woods and lake: invading the marshes, emerging muddy but triumphant with frogs; snatching up toads and brown garter snakes from the grass; shooting their BB guns at crows—with little effect angling for bass at the end of the dock. They even set a trap for eels. Maybe they'd go after the bears while they were at it—Claire wouldn't have been surprised. No doubt it was natural, their predatory curiosity, but she saw something almost frenetic in their activity. Hyperactive, she thought trying to take nature by storm.

Only it better not be her garden. "I see you've got your dog," she said, as the creature, a basic black dog, came bound ing up. "Remember dogs and flowers don't mix."

"Yes, ma'am." They looked at her gravely. "Come on, Pharaoh, heel."

"He doesn't mind much," Kevin said, seizing him by the collar. "But we've got a leash."

"Good boy," she said.

It was taking all Claire's effort to rescue a little plot from the grass since it had become overgrown. In spite of herself, she was appalled at what she'd allowed to happen. The past two summers she'd done nothing but lie about in a stupor, often not getting out of bed till noon, hardly venturing out of doors. Fortunately the lilies were hardy—the grass hadn't choked them out—and even the delphiniums and foxglove had managed to bloom.

Now, at least, she clung to the notion of a garden, though not for what it used to mean to her. These days it was so much grass to pull, so many stones to dig out. You could hardly turn your back before weeds invaded every pause. Her labors left her exhausted. But, now that she was planning to sell the place, she could go to it with a certain fierce resolve. The garden would be a selling point.

And so, my dear, she wrote, turning back to her letter, the letter she was always writing—in her head, if not on **paper** *have the tigers of wrath proved wiser than the horses of instruction?* By all means put your bets on the tigers. They tore their way to something more pure, more real, o fire of wrath, than ever horsely instruction could plod to. Love?—toss aside instruction altogether. *One dark interlude to blot out the love of eighteen years—how could it have happened?*

She paused, uncertain, as she always did before the loss that had depleted her. There had been some tough years, it was true, when Evan had few assignments—something lackluster in his work-and they had to depend mostly on her salary. Was that the beginning of his restlessness, a hint of absence, physical distance? Followed by the summer he'd flung himself uselessly about the camp. Scaring her. She hadn't known how to meet him.

"Why don't you do some photos?" she'd said, thinking that some of his best had come from there. The lake. Swamps. The old decaying train station. Portraits of the old-timers still around. He'd won prizes. He'd published a calendar that made things pretty flush for a while, even taken him to Mexico.

"This place bores me to death." She'd been too stunned to speak. "You don't *move,*" he accused her. "How can you stand it? You're like a frog stuck in its waddy. Don't you know there's a world out there?"

Claire had felt condemned at the source of her being.

What was there to say to him? An image came to mind. Still now in July the dark woods were filled with little lights. Fire flies. Off, on. Lovely, but the dark was still dark. *Was it that you stopped loving me?* Loving who she was, wanting what she was not. She leaned back, her pen having taken her by surprise. Was that why he had kept picking at her, turning all her faults up for inspection? Stripping her of all dignity. Till a tiger, still small, leapt out in spite of her. Surprised him, no doubt. And then it began—the wrath of tigers. Followed by the numbness that even after two years she hadn't been able to dispel, that said she loved him still and hadn't moved beyond that. *I hate love,* she thought.

"Do you know what we saw?" Back so soon, or had they ever left?

"No, what?" Claire said. Who had cast her in the gritty role of patience?

"A moose."

"Two mooses. Only he didn't see the second one. I did," Kevin boasted.

"I did too."

"Okay, boys, trot on home now," she told them, standing up to assume a more commanding position. "Remember, lunchtime.

Let's take a little break." *Dammit,* she thought.

I don't come up here to babysit somebody else's kids. The parents ought to know better.

"Hey, there's a car coming," Kevin said.

Her own kid—she'd been expecting him. Daniel, her one and only. She tried to summon the resources for the occasion. For Maria, her granddaughter, now six, was coming as well. A child she hadn't seen at all during the past two years.

"Let's go see," Kevin said.

"Hold on a minute," Claire said. "This is private."

"Hey, it's Dad," one of the boys yelled, as they went romping around to the front. As Claire went outside, her neighbor climbed out of his Explorer, a roughened version of his older son. As he paused, he gave the impression he had merely stopped to ask for directions.

'I'm John Hurley," he said, approaching. "Your new neighbor." He extended his hand.

"See," Kevin said. "This is the nice lady we told you about." *Nice lady.* Claire winced. Had they badgered him into coming over? She worked up a smile. "It's such a relief to have someone in the camp again," she said. "We were afraid it was going to rack and ruin." We—she caught herself . For so many years they had been together. The habit was ingrained. "I've heard you working over there."

"I think we got it just in time."

No youngster, she could see—in his forties at least. She admired his ambition.

'Tm glad I can do a lot of the work myself, though I've had some help. At least the roof's on and there are no more leaks. The furniture was a wreck."

'I'll bet. You've taken on a real job."

"Good for me," he said. "Therapeutic, as they say."

She wished they wouldn't. Just let them try to tell her that about her garden . . .

"But it'll be great," he added, as though to assure himself.

"We love it here. This lake, the woods." He gestured with open palms.

"Don't forget the loons," Kevin put in.

"And the train," Bradley said. "And the moose."

"I hope they haven't been bothering you," their father said. "They help me a lot when I can corral them. The rest of the time I've pretty much left them on their own." They had claimed him—standing in front of him, linked together by the arm he had on each of their shoulders.

Now was the time to state her complaint, but some instinct kept her from it. They were new, she was on her way out. Why create bad feelings? But where was the female member of the clan? Staying home till all was put to rights? Surely she'd have come up to take its measure, see what was needed. Clearly there was a missing fourth. No wonder all that masculine energy was running loose.

"Okay, boys," the father said, "I've got to go to town for nails."

"Can we eat at McDonald's?"

"Yeah, McDonald's," Bradley chorused. 'I'm tired of peanut butter and jelly. McDonald's, McDonald's."

"Come on then," he summoned them. "You'll have to come over," he said, as they turned to leave, "when we've got the place fit for company."

She gave them a wave. *Oh, don't bother me,* she thought.

Her son arrived later that afternoon. Claire went out to meet him as he emerged from his weathered Honda, worn out by the previous owner—it was a wonder it still ran. He unfolded himself from the front seat, tall and shaggy. He'd grown a beard since she'd last seen him.

Claire hugged him and was stirred by a sense of welcome she was actually glad to see him, though their visit would be difficult. They would come together once again in reminiscence, once again dipping into their history of shared experience. She looked him over. "The beard looks good, but you're too thin. You look like a starving holy man. You haven't been eating."

"Haven't had time," Daniel said, laughing, as he took out first his guitar, then his luggage. One of the battered cases broke open and various books spilled out on the ground—he was always reading half a dozen of them at a time.

"I was hoping you'd bring your guitar," Claire said, as she helped him pick up the books. "But where's Maria? I thought she'd be coming."

"She's in summer camp—Bible camp,"he said with a wince. "She wanted desperately to go—a little friend wanted her company. It was dirt cheap, so I could afford it. I expect I'll be hearing a lot about Jesus. That's over in a week. Then I'll go down and get her, bring her back up. If that's all right with you."

"How could it not be?" Two weeks then, if she could manage it.

"I'm giving a recital in August," he told her. "So I've got to practice. I hope that won't shatter your peace and quiet."

"Like having Segovia for a guest."

"That would be far better."

Modesty, she was convinced, was his undoing, together with his passion for perfection. It was in the logic of things he would take up both some unattainable ideal and the classical guitar— the perfect combination for starving your way through lif e. Playing for some church or civic group, usually to raise funds for a variety of worthy causes—the sort of gig that yielded him a pittance. He gave lessons to other aspirants for the strenuous life. He was thirty-one. In the domestic sphere he had fared little better. There'd been a brief tempestuous relationship with a flamenco dancer, a Spanish girl now doing a tour of nightclubs in Mexico and Latin America. Their child, Maria, was living with him now. Apparently he had the more settled life.

That afternoon the boys were back under her window. She had again picked up her letter while Dan was out for a swim. Half of it she had crossed out.

The two boys had only one small trout between them. But

they were undaunted. "Guess what we saw," Kevin said. "A bear."

"Really," she said. In all her years on the lake she'd caught only one brief glimpse of one.

"It was big and it had teeth like this. And it stood up and came running. It was fierce. Roaring." Kevin demonstrated. "I saw seven deer," Bradley said.

"You did not."

"And a coyote."

"All today?" she asked. "You've been busy." The infantile note struck her, as though they were making their last defenses against a beleaguered childhood.

"Some yesterday," Kevin allowed. "Hey, c'mon," he said to his brother. "We've got frogs to catch if we're going out in the boat." They took off at a trot.

They left the afternoon to settle back into the fullness of light, into the illusion of peace. Claire looked at what she had written. What was the point? Did she really imagine a letter would unite the broken pieces, ignite the old spark? Years ago Dan and the neighbor's girl, Denise, had dived day after day, bringing up pieces of a china pitcher long ago thrown into the lake. When they got it assembled, but for one piece they could never find, and had duly admired it, they threw it all back into the lake. Altogether fitting—like a ceremony. Broken love affairs deserved a similar ritual. Perhaps she was still looking for the missing piece, as though that would restore everything. *What happens to love?* she wondered. *Where does it go when the vessel breaks?*

How many times had she written the letter, crossing things out, changing the wording, recopying it? The same obsessive round. More. It was a punishment. She had locked herself in it and was angry that she'd done so. She folded the paper inside the recipe book she had out and turned her attention to supper. She had someone to cook for again.

"Smells good," Daniel said, when he came in after his swim. He looked around. "This kitchen," he said, as though that summed up the bounty it had offered over the years. "Any hope of a blue-berry pie?"

Of course he was expecting one—it had completely slipped her mind. "There's always hope," she said. "But you'll have to help me pick berries. Maybe I can have one when Maria gets here."

"Have you got the canoe out?"

"No," she said. "I was waiting for you." It was a lie. She'd lacked all ambition.

Daniel sat down at the table to watch as Claire made corn bread. When she caught him unawares, he looked haggard. She hesitated to ask him anything specific about his present circumstances. There was the recital—good enough. "So how've things been going?" she said. "You like your new spot?"

"I did pretty well early in the summer, and I'm getting a rep-utation. But it's not like Irish music or bluegrass. Something you can do in a pub any weekend." He paused. "I saw Dad."

"Oh," Claire said.

"I hope that doesn't bother you."

She shrugged. She seldom allowed herself to think about him any more. "I never disliked your father. It's just that *work* was a dirty word to him."

"Well, I know you went through a lot." It was generous of Dan. No doubt he'd gone through a few things himself. "It's pretty much the same. He was doing okay as a night watchman, but things got dull, and he invited over some of his friends . . ."

She sighed. "Same as ever." Everybody loved the man; he was God's gift to conviviality.

He'd probably needed money and given Dan one of his des-perate phone calls, and Dan had given him what he could ill af-ford and would never see again. Dan, of course, would never ask Claire for money—he'd starve first. She had to find ways of slip-ping him a little extra. That's the way it had always been.

They dropped the subject, and he then asked for news of the lake people he'd known over the years: Who had been up this summer, who'd gotten married among his circle, who had babies? Nell, she told him, had come through her bout with cancer—that was a relief. The Davises were off to Machu Picchu, would be up later in the summer. Despite distance and absence he'd forgotten nothing of their friends and acquaintances. He spoke of Clyde and Evelyn and Bea and Dolly as if he'd seen them only last week and brought up anecdotes she'd all but forgotten.

When they'd reached the end of the news and gossip, she primed herself for what had to come.

"You know," she said in a low voice, 'I'm putting the place up for sale."

"I was hoping it wouldn't come to that," he said. So he'd preceded her in the thought.

Surprised by grief, she felt tears spring to her eyes. For love gone awry or for the simple fact of change—that things were no longer what they'd been. "You know how I loved it here. But now . . ."

He stood up and put his arms around her.

"You know, I think about this place—how I was the one who wanted it, who put up a fuss. Mom and Dad had absolutely no interest in it, and of course your uncle hated any thing that wasn't the city. If it hadn't been for me it would have been sold in five minutes."

"I know," he said. "I can't even imagine what my life would have been without being here."

"Only now without Evan . . ."

"The way he treated you . . ." Claire could tell that he was holding in his anger.

"I never tried to hold him here," she wept. "He went off to Mexico that time. I always told him to do what he needed to do."

"I don't think it's that," Dan said.

"Then what? Somebody younger?"

"He's had to acknowledge he's gone as far as he can go. That's not always easy."

"Perhaps he wanted too much."

"Like everybody."

She had no answer. "Every time I turn around I'm over come by memories—they leap out of every corner. Even these dishes, every variety of Willow Ware imaginable, that we've always eaten on. How many hundreds of meals. It's unbearable. And it's all gone—with nothing left."

"Not quite," he countered. "You're here right now making cornbread. If Vermeer were around, he'd paint you standing there, right in that window with the light on your face. Cap turing just this moment. *You* haven't changed."

But it wasn't the right moment: a particular configuration of sky and water and Evan coming in triumphant with photos he'd taken or the fish he'd caught. And she, light and transparent as air.

"Oh, come now," she said. "Don't give me that. Look at me," she insisted. "Can't you see how diminished? I just wonder— Love," she said with scorn. "Whoever invented it? What a dumb idea. And what does it get you?"

He gave a little ironic laugh. "Experience," he said. "Well, leave me out of it."

He stood silently, rubbing her shoulder.

"Oh, go on," she said, stepping back and wiping her eyes. "You're just making me angry. No, it's not you. I should be past all the nonsense. Every time I read a newspaper I think wars and plagues and crime and hunger—all this grief and suffering, and me with my little atom. Why is it such a torment?"

"Because you live and breathe—how's that for starters?"

"Yes, well, attachment—what we're all supposed to be rid of. I'll never settle for resignation," she said. "I never imagined you would."

"Go on," she said. "I've got to shell peas."

"You want help?"

"No," she said. "Just go. It's good for me to do something absolutely mindless." *Like digging in the dirt,* she thought.

He went off to read until supper was ready, lying in the living room on the old couch with the springs coming through.

She turned her attention to supper—the potatoes, the peas, the fish. The steps, the right order. It was supposed to be a relief to tell him she was going to sell the place. And he hadn't reproached her. Only now she was in greater turmoil than ever, as though she were betraying—what? But then what was she supposed to do—hold onto her grief as though it were a collector's item? The tapestry gets torn and you stare into the gaping hole. *Riddle me this: when is nothing better than something?*

When she went to call Daniel to supper, she saw he had fallen asleep, arm flopped down beside him, book lying on the floor. She bent down to pick it up, to see what he was pursuing just now, in his perennial desire to know everything. She glanced at the open page. "O wonder!" she read. "A garden amid fires. I have followed love like a camel. My heart is capable of every form."

Bully for him. And who was it—she glanced at the cover that could boast of such a sentiment? Not of this world. How had he managed to survive in mere flesh and blood? Hanging by a thread no doubt, like Daniel. The name of the author was unfamiliar to her.

"Supper's ready," she said.

"Oh, I fell asleep," Daniel said, sitting up. "Funny—I was dreaming about how we used to come up here when the Wheatleys still had the fishing camp. Remember that girl Serene, the one who used to get all the letters from her boy friends? I had such a crush on her. Always wondered what happened to her."

"She ran off with old McCain, you remember him, the handyman who worked over there."

"Really? When did you learn that? He must have been seventy-five!"

"Lily Wheatley told me. No, come to think of it, a couple of old-timers came around to visit . . ."

He shook his head. "She was something to look at," he said, "but of course she never cast an eye in my direction."

The boys were back again the next weekend. They'd been by several times to show their various trophies. Now, late in the afternoon, she saw them troop by her garden, their dog trailing behind them. They were in serious conversation.

"Aunt Billie said I shouldn't masturbate," Bradley said. "What does that mean?"

"It means when you play with yourself."

"Oh."

So we come to knowledge, she thought. She had been alone for the day. Daniel had gone down to Portland to pick up Maria and would return possibly that night, but more likely the next afternoon. She had put in her time in the garden. The coneflowers were coming along, as well as the coreopsis and pincushions. The lilies were opening. She had gotten out most of the grass and fertilized the plants. It looked good, she had to admit. Next she turned to the shelves in the living room, still full of the games and kids' books that Dan and his friends had grown up with. *All this stuff,* she thought. What ever had she been keeping it for? A few of the books and some of the simpler games and puzzles she put aside for Maria. The rest would get the heave-ho. Then as she picked up two puzzles, the sort that have a thousand and one pieces, she immediately knew what to do with them. They might even keep the kids out of her hair for a while.

She took the path through the woods to her new neighbors and found the three of them on the porch, the boys bent in concentration over a jammed fishing reel.

"Come in, come in," John Hurley said, clearly pleased to see her.

"I was cleaning out some shelves and thought the boys might like these."

They looked up, eager. "Hey, that's great," Kevin said, taking them, looking over the pictures on the lids. The reel was abandoned. "Come on," he said to his brother. "We can set up the card table."

"Thanks a lot," John Hurley said. "We had been living off

card tables, but we just got this for the porch." He indicated the oak table the boys had risen from. "And there's a new table in the kitchen too."

"Molly's First Hand Second Hand?"

"You got it. I've been her prime customer this month. New mattresses, divan—the works. Come inside, I'll show you around."

Indeed the place had been transformed. The kitchen/living room was newly paneled with pine; a shine came from the new linoleum on the floor. On the stove something appetizing was cooking in a Dutch oven. A loaf of bread that looked to be home-made rested on a cutting board. The bedrooms at the back were neatly arranged with beds and bureaus. The boys already had the card table set up and were laying out the pieces. Comfort. Order. Her eye was drawn to a small silver framed photograph in which a woman stood with John Hurley and the two boys, smiling an odd slanting smile Claire found rather winning, if poignant—her hair apparently ruffled by a strong breeze. It occurred to Claire she had focused on a point of reference, that all she saw had been done with this woman in mind.

"I remember this camp being awfully dark," Claire said. "I see you've put in a skylight."

"I also took down a couple of trees that blocked out the light. They're stacked up in back for firewood."

"What a lot you've accomplished."

"I took a couple of weeks off just after we bought the camp, and then my brother gave me a hand. Sit down. I've been at it all day, and I could use a breather. Could I interest you in a gin and tonic?"

"I should be getting back," Claire said automatically, then thought, *Well, why not?* Hell, she could use a drink. "But you've tempted me—" She sat in the chair he offered her. "You have such a fine view here," she said, "right on the water."

"Yes," he said. "You can see the whole lake now. Once I got those branches down, everything opened up."

He had his domain, took pride in what he could do for him self.

The roof he had fixed, the lake he had brought into view, very likely whatever was cooking in the pot on the stove. Maybe he was using her for practice, to show what he could offer. A wife-price for the missing one. He went back into the kitchen and mixed drinks for both of them.

Before she knew it they'd talked away the rest of the afternoon. While the sun was dropping and a little wind was kicking up on the lake, they'd been deep into the local history, who had come and gone over the years. He kept asking her questions; one thing led to another, and she had gone through a whole range of incident and anecdote, things she'd been repeating for years: the time she and her neighbor, with the help of Dan and friend, had tried to cook a huge snapping turtle in a copper washtub. "Stunk up the whole place," she said. "But the meat was quite tasty." The time the train had derailed, cars with Bunker C oil spilling over the woods, a tank car of gasoline catching fire. How everyone had fled and watched the smoke rising from the shore, certain the whole place would go up in flames. The summer Tim Johnson's Cessna had plunged into the treetops just after it took off—in front of a group of horrified friends gathered to wave him off. Somehow Tim and his son emerged from the woods with only a few scratches, the branches having broken the fall.

As the sun dropped and the lake was again turning to stillness, it was as though she were handing him the book in which he would begin to fill out his own page.

He considered. "I think being here will do Jenny a world of good. My wife," he added.

"That's her picture inside?"

"Yes," he said. "She's been having a rough time." He didn't elaborate.

'I'm sorry," she said.

He shrugged. "One of those things . . . But she'll pull out of it." He paused. 'I'm sure of it. Here," he said, taking her glass. "let me get you another."

"I won't be able to make it home." Somehow she was in no hurry to leave.

"The boys and I can carry you," he said, with a laugh. "I've just been enjoying our conversation."

"Dad," Kevin said, coming up. "Can she stay and have supper with us?"

"I was just about to ask."

She looked at her watch. "Good heavens, it's almost seven."
"We'd love to have you," he said. "You'll save us from leftovers. Think of it as a golden deed."

"Stay, stay," Bradley pleaded.

They were going to accompany her back to her camp, but she insisted she could find her way alone; she'd been a child here, she reminded them. She'd been in every inch of these woods. She did accept one of their flashlights. But she could have found her way without it. There was moonlight, and the stars were thick. She could see the Big Dipper and the stars in Orion's belt. Her grandfather had taught her the constellations. His telescope was still there in the camp, the satin lining of the case a bit rusty looking. And fireflies flickered through the trees, winked in the grass. Every year it was the same . . . Every July, disappearing in August. Ever since she'd started coming, her grandfather driving down to Bangor to pick her up. Then her first excited view of the lake that had waited for her return. Reflections of the trees in the water, the infinite lights and shades, clouds drifting over, shifting shape.

She slapped a mosquito on her arm. Another whined at her head. Mosquitoes and blackflies—always there too. Frog voices edged the night. For a couple of years there'd been no sound of them, but now the frogs were back. A loon called across the lake, two short notes and a long haunting one. Answering calls, giggles. Echoes filled the cove. She couldn't imagine the lake without its loons. Or without the deer and moose, even the blackflies and mosquitoes. Inexhaustible nature. Seen by her eyes and the eyes of all the rest. Always the same and yet always different in the various strands of sensation and consciousness that held it alltogether. The widest net was all of it, the source and the thing itself. Generation and demise, gathering and dividing.

A strain of music waltzed around in her head. After their meal of Irish stew and slabs of bread and butter, the kids had gone back to their puzzle; and she and John Hurley had lingered over coffee and sat watching an early moon over the lake.

"I think we need some music," he said, and went to put a tape into the tape player on the kitchen floor.

A moment later she was hearing Glenn Miller's "In the Mood."

"That goes back a way," she said.

"I'm glad the big bands are coming around again," he said.

"I always liked this piece." He made a little bow in her direction. "Could I interest you in a little dancing?"

"I haven't danced in years," she said, standing up. It was an odd request in the middle of the woods, but why not? He put his hand on her waist, they joined hands, and he led her into the music.

"I just got a tape of the New Swing," he said, "but it sounds very much like the Old Swing to me."

"I was mad about dancing when I was in high school and college."

They dropped all talk and turned their attention to movement and music. He held her lightly, a little pressure signal ing the way they would move. It was dark outside now, the lake a lighter dark than the silhouetted trees. It didn't matter that they had to maneuver around the table and chairs. He led her across the threshold into the kitchen and then back out onto the porch. It was easier than she thought, the rhythm of dancing still in her feet. Their eyes caught in the effort of con centration, everything else stripped away but that. A certain fluidity carried them, a tac-it intimacy they were unlikely to repeat.

When the piece finished, neither moved to sit down, but waited for the next tune. They glided into "You Can't Take That away from Me." He was humming at her ear. Afterward they hugged each other, breathless and laughing.

"That was wonderful," he said.

Dancing in the middle of the woods. Wonderful! And what was she practicing for, she wondered, having risen to the touches of sensation, the potential attraction that could light up anywhere? It was too late for that now. She had proceeded to the aftermath, gone to the other side of desire. And what sort of territory was that?

She noticed as she passed alongside the garden that the lights were on in the camp. Daniel must have arrived. Maria would be there. She wondered how long they'd been waiting for her. She heard his voice:

"Time for bed, Maria. Come in now."

She met him as he was moving in Maria's direction with a flashlight.

"Oh, hello. Where've you been?"

"Just down to the new neighbors' cabin. I wasn't expecting you."

He laughed. "We had to come up tonight. Maria absolutely insisted."

"What's she doing?"

"Catching lightning bugs—what else? I think kids can see in the dark like cats."

"How about it, sweetie?" he called. "Grandma's here."

"Hi, Grandma," she heard from down the path. "I just came."

"The mosquitoes are fierce," she said. "I hope she won't get eaten alive."

"I put some spray on. She slept most of the way up, and I thought I could get her to bed without her waking. Boy, was I wrong. She had to have a jar and go out this very minute." Claire could see Maria's indistinct form among the trees.

A silhouette that could have been hers at that age, two shadows blending one into the other, out in the same woods on the same mission. Green lights in a glowing jar. Could you read by them?

And here she was coming, her face carrying its own light surrounded by dark curls, two teeth missing in front.

"Look, Grandma," she said, running up. "See, I've caught one."

Carnival for the Gods

It was the first time Dusty had ever backhanded her, and it was not just the blow, the pain, the blood from her lip flowing saltily into her mouth that gave Alta the shock: it was the sense that something fatal had struck at the roots of her life. Things would never be the same. It was the edge of Dusty's ring that had cut her lip, a gold ring with a strange little head carved in ivory that he'd bought during a fit of extravagance in Kansas City and said was his good luck and that he'd never part with it. As she stood in the cramped little bathroom, looking into the mirror, teeth all outlined in red as though she'd been eating red-hearted plums or pomegranates, the lip still bleeding, it seemed as though she'd never staunch the flow. This is my life, she thought; this is time leaking away, as it has been doing year upon year. And I'm standing here letting it happen like I was born without a brain.

The whole of the little trailer had shaken with their quarrel, till even words and the clash of voices could not contain the violence. Pansy, the little curly-haired dog she kept, a cross between a poodle and a wire-haired terrier, had taken refuge under the couch and, looking at Alta with brown eyes that seemed full of the light of tragedy, still refused to come out. Dusty meanwhile had thrown himself out of the trailer and into the truck, banging doors all the way, setting up a cloud of dust as he roared off into town, leaving her there alone with the freaks and the animals in the broken-down carnival. She dabbed at her lip as she tried to calm her feelings. She was looking pretty terrible at the moment. Face blotched, bags under her eyes, broken lip, but she wasn't all that old—forty-seven—and there was still a chance for ... what? For love, for money?

Money talks—she'd learned that much. It says *yes* and it says *no*. Says, *you owe it to yourself, baby; go on and have it. Be my guest*. Says, *you're out of luck, sister. Says, go to the city and have yourself a ball*; says, *stay home and starve your gut.* Says, *turn on the gold-plated faucet, break out the champagne.* Says, *stay away, lady, you smell bad, and nobody's gonna give you a second look.* Says, *dream—the sky's the limit.* Says, *look at the walls peeling.* Says, *go hang yourself.*

It says, Alta concluded, *you have been with a man who's brought you nothing but trouble and grief, all the while promising you the world.* And where has it landed you? Down in the flatlands with blood on your teeth. Always full of harebrained schemes. And he wasn't half as crazy as the rest of the outfit, only more unreliable.

"I'm sick of this life. Filled up to here." That's how it had begun. Dusty, sitting at the narrow formica-topped table with the bench on either side, at which they had shared what might be called their domestic life, was adding up one of his interminable columns of figures. Always trying to turn nothing into something, as Alta had it, to make less come out to be more. "Sick of it." He looked up: "There's no anchor hanging out of your ass."

The truth of this observation left her momentarily speechless—a yawl in a dead wind. Then her fury unlidded, and the fine brew the years had whipped to froth came boiling over, pouring out: the salt was in her mouth, the distillation of years of sweat and tears and gall. All she might have had—all that had gone down the drain.

It was the sandstorm that finally did it to her. Bad enough to have the equipment truck break down in the flattest, most god-forsaken stretch of natural freakishness she'd ever laid eyes on. Like somebody's uninteresting nightmare. A world created out of what any sensible being would've rejected in the first place or else reached for only in the dry heaves of violent boredom: things twisted and sharp and spiny and hard. Some of them reached up and out with arms dried and dead in their attitudes of empty aspiration. They seemed neither plant nor tree, these cacti and joshua trees; nor alive, these clutches of dry grass and sage brush against a rocky ground that gave off a hard glint. The rocks that rose in the distance looked to have no living thing growing on them. Only telephone poles and the blacktop to show that human beings had been here, mainly,

Alta thought, to get through it and on to somewhere else: the sort of place you might consider beautiful only if you didn't have to be there.

It was one of those undistinguished spots of blacktop, miles from the notion of a town, they'd come to a halt in the middle of, when the rear axle of the equipment truck broke down, and their little procession came to an uneven halt, like train cars piling up. There was a dull, angry look in the sky, and they'd no sooner got their vehicles pulled off onto the shoulder than the wind picked up the dust and flung it at them, striking the metal roofs and sides like a flail. It was a good thing they weren't going anywhere, because they couldn't have seen to get there anyway. The sun was eclipsed, the windows dark with dust. And though the doors and windows were shut, so they were nearly stifled inside, the dust sifted through anyway, a fine layer over everything. They drank it in their coffee and ate it with their food.

The animals nearly went crazy. The horses neighed and tried to rear in their trailer. The little elephant stamped and trumpeted. The tiger paced her cage all night. And what with the fray and the clatter, the bay gelding had somehow injured a leg. They needed both a vet and a mechanic, two more bills to pay. So it was no wonder that on this day, in what appeared to be the wreckage of the storm, most of the people in the show pulled out. The operators of the booths——little independent outfits that had hooked up with them and would hook on somewhere else. The shooting gallery left, and the lucky spinning wheel, the car races, the coin and ring tossing set-ups——most of the acts and all the games of chance were taking their chances elsewhere.

"Well, you gotta live," Pearl Diamond said when she and Bates, who threw knives at her till her silhouette stood outlined upon the wall and she stepped forth unscathed, were taking off. "Be seeing you," they said to Alta. "No hard feelings." The first to leave, they had put the idea into the common mind, though no doubt somebody else would have thought of it too. Any woman, Alta thought, who trusted a man enough to allow him to throw knives at her was either too dumb or too lucky to have troubles in the world, and she envied her even as she wished her well.

If they hadn't missed the turn-off, probably none of this would have happened. They were supposed to have headed north towards Albuquerque, but they'd missed the sign and hadn't had the sense God gave a turnip to stop and look at a map. Before they knew it, they'd gone fifty miles out of their way.

If you hadn't . . . And how are we going to get out of this godforsaken place? Money and blame. *Bitch, bitch, bitch. As if a man hasn't got enough troubles . . . Whose idea was it to . . . ? As if you never made a mistake . . .* Money and blame. *I could've made fifty to your one, and we'd both be better off.* Brick bats flying back and forth. *Pulling your weight . . . Whose weight . . . Fed up with your... Because of you, godammit. You gave me nothing, not even a child . . . Couldn't plant anything in that belly of yours except a fart . . . I should've got me a better man to try.*

The blood had dried on her lip. Tentatively she touched the spot, then turned from the mirror. *I could've been . . .* Not been—was. Was one of the best damn trapeze artists in the business. The two of them together: Gold Dust and Dream Girl. The dream had turned to dust—hah! Ashes to ashes: Gold Dust to Dusty, what a joke. The two of them one great act, till the moment suddenly came, maybe by a slip of the foot and one miss in midair too many, by too dizzying a glance down below, Dusty seemed to lose his nerve, wanted to settle for a life on the ground, but with higher ambitions: a show of his own. At the time when they could've had top billing in "The Greatest Show on Earth," Dusty chased his dream of something grander yet, circus and carnival together, triumphantly called "The Carnival for the Gods." Earth wasn't enough for him.

He was headed into the clouds, into the skyscape of the forever possible, the shape of things to come. They'd play all the big cities, bringing back the days when everybody went to the circus. Giant celebrations in the heart of every city.

But the idea never really got off the ground. It was too vast for anybody but Dusty to believe in for very long. The force of his enthusiasm—he could talk people into anything and they would follow him around with puppylike loyalty—held them for awhile. But starvation was a powerful eye-opener. The shine wore off and off they went. And now they were down to the rag, taggle and bob that had stayed because they had nowhere else to go.

There had been better days: when she was up on the high wire, and her body was a flash of motion as she swung, hanging by her heels, across the top of the tent, the faces below like rows of lightbulbs, her body light as a firefly in her blue body suit. All alone up there, no nets below, with the tight thrill that was the joy bred of danger. The tingle in the blood. God, how she loved it! It was the years that had brought her down to earth. She'd nearly killed herself once in a fall. She'd lost her timing, her body had gotten heavy despite all her efforts. The pull of gravity, the reluctance of the flesh. And all the while Dusty trying to put together his misbegotten scheme.

She put some water in the kettle to boil and took out ajar of Sanka. She didn't like the taste much, but even with the heat it was something to put into your mouth and swallow. Something to look into and stir your spoon around in while you sat. She spooned out the instant, poured in the water and sat ruminating, waiting for the coffee to cool, gazing into the dark liquid. Time out. It allowed you to sit down right in the midst of life while somewhere else people were killing each other or having babies or getting the mortgage foreclosed or carrying on a family quarrel that would leave seven people sworn enemies for life. Set a cup of coffee in front of you and none of it mattered, at least for the moment; otherwise you were out scratching and biting and clawing because the world was an obstacle you had to strike out at.

She was full of yearning, but she didn't know what for. When she had had money, she bought clothes, strange fanciful outfits that could have taken her to another age and fashion, or to a costume party. She loved bodices decorated with pearls and sequins and fringes that shimmied when you walked and rhinestones that danced the light. She loved bright colors: reds that could have come from the throat of a trumpet and pinks and oranges and purples that peeled your eyeball back to the optic nerve. She had trousers and a turban made of cloth of gold, and tops all embroidered. Even now, when she took tickets she sometimes dressed up as the Queen of Sheba or a priestess of the moon in a gown, her special creation, that shimmered between gold and silver, set off by a crown of rhinestones with a fan of feathers rising from the back. But nobody paid any special attention. She had the stuff all packed in the closet. And Dusty wanted her to get rid of all that rubbish, just taking up space, but it would have been like stripping off her own skin. Yet she knew she'd never wear them anymore. Most of them were too tight anyway.

No, money wasn't good for anything. It was good to spend when you had it, but then you tossed aside what you had bought as so much junk. Dusty still had his ring—so much for the luck it had brought him.

As for love, that was even worse. Had she loved Dusty, she wondered, or had she just wanted a man who dreamed big, was headed for the clouds?

He couldn't even give her a child.

Small wonder he had time to put the makings in her belly, considering where his head always was: scheming and dreaming and adding up columns of figures and charting their course around the country and talking half the night away, too excited even to make love. And though there were ups as well as downs at the beginning, things now were headed in one direction only. It didn't seem to occur to him that they were all washed up. The gaggle of folks they'd picked up was the rout, the survivors who hadn't quite gone over the edge, not the glittering argosy he'd always had in mind. A man with a dream was a madman.

Love. Much worse than money. A giant and a midget who fought and were inseparable. An animal trainer who was convinced a woman lived inside his tiger, the only woman he'd ever wanted. Idly, she wondered if anybody had ever tried fucking a tiger. She'd heard about doing it with cows and sheep and dogs. Probably even with trees, provided you weren't so unlucky as to strike upon a bee hive inside. For all of which, she thought, you'd have to be pretty damn desperate. But a tiger. Even if you could get one to stand still for it, there was something in the nature of a cat that ought to make you a bit leery. You couldn't put your dependence on them. But then the trainer, Sam, was nuts too. Love was too much. It created bizarre obsessions. It was a form of drunkenness and self-abuse. They threatened you with blindness if you twiddled your own organs, or with impotence or insanity. But they should've been smarter than that. Love itself was blind and impotent, insane, and ate the heart away until it was white and leprous and scarred beyond all telling. Never trust it, she thought.

Every once in a while when she needed to feel a little pride in herself, she got dolled up and ran off to have an affair with a truck driver or salesman or drifter who was looking for a little diversion. Men she didn't count on seeing again and usually didn't—or, if she did, the interest had passed. She used to like the thrill in the blood of having a new man, but even that had got old. She didn't trust it anymore, no more than she trusted a greenback. No, neither love nor money had taken her anywhere—just left her here tasting her own blood.

She wanted vaguely to kill somebody, but there wasn't anybody handy and certainly nobody worth the trouble. If it wasn't love and it wasn't money . . . The blood was beating in her veins. It went on beating and beating. Blood, sweat and tears—maybe *they* were real. She found the water running out of her eyes. Real as dirt. Till you were dirt too. They'd discovered America, and what was it but dirt? She looked outside. The dust had blown off and under the blaze of sun the land was cooking into a piece of burnt toast. Maybe she should go out and start digging, see if she could strike oil. Wouldn't that be a humdinger!

Or maybe she should pull herself together and get up and leave like everybody else. She and Dusty had fought and torn at each other, had driven and goaded and disappointed one another nearly as far as human things can go. And now he'd made her taste her own blood, and she was still here. And what if from now on he made a pleasure of beating on her? Or if she stood for it . . . It made no sense. And if she left . . . what would she do? Go wandering through the world, probably, only by herself, waitressing at some cafe or bar. Trying to cadge drinks and lure men home. Even now there'd be snickers behind her back, not to think of the future.

She got up from the table and gave herself to the task of fixing supper: cut up meat and fried it with sliced onions and put in the tomatoes and chili peppers and set the pot on the stove to cook. What with the mechanic and the vet costing an arm and a leg, it might be the crew's last good meal for a while. Every time you took somebody a car or a body it seemed they wanted you to set them up for life. She'd make a big pot of chili that would either tide them over for a couple of days or feed whoever happened to wander in. Once she'd done that, she washed her face and cleaned herself up a little. She was needing company. She'd see what Billy Bigelow was up to.

She could count on him. He'd been with them forever, first as electrician, carpenter, handyman, what-have-you, and now, after the defection of Carnaby the Great, he was featured as Bigelow the Magician. He could pull cards from out of people's pockets and from behind their ears and discover scarves where they hadn't been before. He had mastered appearance and disappearance and seemed to want to climb to ever higher steps of illusion. Though sometimes he would simply take a pile of long thin balloons and blow them up, twist them into dogs and lions and elephants and kangaroos and send them sailing out into the crowd.

She found him sitting on the couch in his trailer reading a *Time* magazine. Probably months or a year old, since Billy never bought one. But the dates never interested him, it never mattered to him when an event had occurred.

"Dream Girl," he said, "come on in." He was the only person who ever called her that, and it seemed to be the only image he'd ever had of her: up in the air on the high wire. If it were anybody else, she'd be convinced she was being made fun of.

"Been looking at some moon shots they got here. All crust and craters."

"My God, why don't you look out the window? Isn't that desolate enough for you? If you get up and go outside, you could be on part of the moon they haven't discovered yet. The lower part."

"You really think the moon looks like this," he asked.

"If it don't, it's missed a bet." She'd come over to joke a bit, but the direction the conversation was taking her, making her think about where she was, only brought on her irritability. She wished Dusty would come back so she could throw something at him.

"You know what I think?" Billy said, taking off his glasses so he could see her more clearly. "I think they go out and take all those pictures and say it's the moon."

"Why'd they do a thing like that? Besides, you got all those rockets going up and men coming down in capsules and stuff."

"Oh, you could fake that." Billy said, with a snap of the fingers. "No trouble at all. Just take a picture, put it alongside another and say it's the moon."

"What on earth for?"

"Because you got to keep one step ahead of the public. You got to keep them wondering, always in suspense. Otherwise they'd get so bored and dull in their minds they'd turn back into tree frogs. There they'd be, rocking back and forth going mumbledyboo and their eyes would go crossed and their lips would droop and pretty soon they'd be squatting in clusters like fungus, just trying to keep the burner going so life wouldn't go out altogether."

"You got some imagination."

"No, I mean it. That's why you got to have carnivals. Probably they got a secret genius agency somewhere with people that do nothing all day and night but think things up, one leap ahead of the rest of us."

"But all you're talking about is plain lies."

"Of course. What other kind is there? Except some lies are plainer than others. People need them, couldn't get along without them. Think about what people have believed, beginning with the earth being flat. All you have to do is get it into their heads and then they swear it's true."

"But now look," she said. "Nobody really believes you find cards behind their ears."

"They'd like to. And if you could convince them you got some leetle secret, they'd believe that too."

He was always playing these games with himself, and she loved the way he twisted everything around till you didn't know whether you were coming or going. She'd lost all her anger. "Well, if everything can be a lie," she said, "then everything can be true just as well." She hadn't the faintest idea what she meant.

"Because people believe it? Then anything can be the truth, can't it? Like all that stuff about living past lives. That could be true."

"Suppose it is. I can't say it isn't. I can't say people haven't been on the moon."

"The people from the future would be living right now, wouldn't they?"

"And how would you know?"

"Use your head. It's got to follow," he said. "And suppose you could go back to the past and you killed your grandfather, would you be alive now?"

"Of course not," she said offhandedly, even though she knew she was being had.

"But then how could you go back. . . ?"

"Why weren't you born with two heads?" she wanted to know. "Then one of you could live in the past and the other in the future and tell each other all about it.

"Probably fell flat on my face," he said, "and the present would go leaking through."

"Through the hole in your head." She stopped, all used up. "How come you don't leave like the rest?"

"The show must go on," he said.

"Come on," she said. "What show? This flea-bitten, half-assed . . . "I love you, Alta—you have such a high opinion of we serious professionals." She couldn't tell if he were teasing her or making fun of himself, or maybe both at once. "I'm a magician."

"And an electrician and a carpenter and—"

"A man of parts," he said.

"Is one of 'em a stomach," she asked. "I've got chili cooking."

"Gotcha."

Back in the trailer she stirred the chili, added some oregano and cumin and then sat down to look at the copy of *Vogue* she'd slipped out of the dentist's office the time she had a toothache in Biloxi.

The sun had really turned on the juice, so she tried to get a little relief by opening the window and turning on the fan. But the flies came in through a tear in the screen and buzzed around her head, and Pansy sat and snapped at them. Now and then she glanced out the window to watch Fred taking care of his horses. He'd taken them out of the trailer one by one and tethered them over by some scrub cedar. He'd brought out hay and water and then had lingered in the heat, grooming them, talking to them, trying to soothe them and make up for a life that offered no explanations, just endless travel, unexpected stops, dust storms, injury and inconvenience—all for the sake of those few triumphant moments in the ring when Ginger, his wife, leapt and danced across their backs.

Every now and then a car or a truck would come whooshing past with a rush of hot air and a slash of light, then go plummeting on into the distance. She had no idea when Dusty would be back. Maybe he'd just taken off like the others. Then a truck—not his—appeared, slowed and finally stopped across the road from the horse trailer. A lean, wiry man got out, took a leather bag from the seat and walked over to where Fred was working with his horses. The vet. As she watched them, a couple of tow trucks pulled up and parked. A burly man, T-shirt sticking to his chest, sunglasses, got out. Then a tall guy, cap on his head, long arms, big hands. Burt, their equipment man, emerged from the rig and came over to talk to them. Then a lot of backing and maneuvering, hauling of chains and attachments. And after a time they were towing the truck away in the direction of what she supposed was a town, though more than likely nothing more than a mirage. She'd believe it when she saw it. But no Dusty.

Then the vet was gone too, and she watched Fred lead the horses back into the trailer. That done, he walked over to the trailer where he lived with Ginger, who leapt from one horse to the other while they raced round the ring, who went up into a handstand or did a flip at the height of their motion, who was beautiful to watch. There was a lightness in her. They deserved better, Alta knew. They were young and, like everybody else who'd been drawn in, had the dream painted in their heads. All full of enthusiasm. Dusty's dream was their dream. She'd seen it happen over and over again. And he wasn't lying when he went on painting the sky in vivid colors. He believed every word of it: it was going to happen. Then, one day, they woke up. He owed them money, like he owed everybody money.

Now she knew they were leaving too. She didn't get up to say goodbye, though she and Ginger had sat in each other's trailers and traded intimacies. And Ginger had showed her bruises on her body in places that didn't show. And sometimes she'd wept: Fred was fonder of his horses than he was of her, treated them better. And to tell the truth, she was sick of the smell of horse. Fred always smelled of horse. Alta didn't go over to say goodbye, because chances were they'd come across each other when they least expected it. In this business you were never surprised.

She felt bad about the money, but there was no help for it. If their paths did cross and Dusty were flush, he'd pay off. That's what he said, and she had no reason to doubt him because so far Dusty hadn't had any money. She watched Ginger climb into the cab of the trailer while Fred went back to drive the one with the horses. Then they were gone. Why wasn't she leaving with them? Was one kind of wandering any worse than another?

For a time she sat there blank and empty, all used up. The anger of the morning seemed as far away as last month. She wasn't even waiting for anything. She turned off the chili, then let the evening move in around her. She sat with her dog in her lap. The deepening sky was a rich blue, a mingling of blues, lighter and dark, with a smoky feeling underneath; it came down into the landscape, softening the edges of the mountains, turning brown slopes to lavender, to indigo, to darker shapes yet that made all of it one vast stillness that reached far beyond her, perhaps to the borders of the world. There were only the little lights of the few trailers left: animal trainer, giant and midget, magician-cum-handyman. That was the carnival now—the scrapings from the pot.

From out of the indigo she saw headlights approach, then heard a truck pull up and stop. She went outside. Dusty was back, but with somebody with him in the front seat. She bent down, leaning on the side of the truck to look in. A girl. She could just about make her out in the gathering dusk. Though she looked to be no more than seventeen-eighteen, she knew everything a woman could know and then some.

"This is Grace," Dusty said, by way of introduction. "Amazing Grace. Wait'll you see what she can do. We'll hit the bigtime yet." I know what she can do, Alta thought. Amazing, all right. Probably one of those street kids that had left home at twelve or thirteen, soon as their periods started and they had their union card for womanhood. Then they peddled it on every street of Everytown in the great U.S. of A. Double A for Amazing. Then she noticed a childish face in the narrow seat behind Dusty. A boy. But so wild he looked like some creature that had been torn away from the land and still carried in its eyes the reflection of the water hole from which it drank, the snug of the nest where it had spent the night still clinging to the fine white hairs on his arms.

"Does he talk?" she suddenly asked.

"The words have gone out of him," the girl said, "but the singing has stayed behind. He knows the ballad of Kitty Moreno and Amigo and the Battle of Glorieta Pass and Indian Joe and his fight with a bear and the loves of Pajarito."

These are barely human things, Alta found herself thinking, for she had learned to recognize such and they were not new to her experience. And here was another set in front of her that she might look at and talk to and never understand. She could ask questions till her teeth rotted and it wouldn't make a ghost of a difference. There they were, almost cringing in the seat of the truck. In the back with the boy, she noticed two crates that looked to be the dimensions of their personal property and inside which something stirred and moved with a vaguely animal and somewhat sinister quality. She didn't ask what.

"You want something to eat," she asked, for she could recognize hunger too, though on what level she couldn't always tell. "I've got a pot of chili on the stove."

They stepped out of the truck, the girl rubbing her arms against the evening chill. Alta saw a square of light as the door of Billy Bigelow's trailer opened. He'd be coming too.

She looked off into the distance before she went inside: over in the mountains it looked as though a storm was brewing up. A sudden flash of lightning and the mountains stood out, every slope and draw outlined in angular crossings of brilliance. If it rains, she thought, it will pick up the dust and the sky will fall down in mud. First they'd nearly been swept away, now it was more than likely they'd be mired down. Or else the water could come tearing down the mountains in a flash flood.

"Come on inside," she said, and went to the stove to put the fire on. Dusty was still fiddling outside in the truck while these two stood uncertainly in the doorway. "You can wash up in there," she said. The boy's eyes went roaming around the trailer as if it would take getting used to. Alta went about setting the table.

Here they were, just another pair among the number she had seen in the procession of all the broken, ill-formed, misbegotten things headed out of the world and onto the road, moving from town to town, never calling any place their own. They were her family, if you could call it that—they were her fate.

She closed the front door. It was getting cold now as night took over the desert. She was closing the door against the night, against the rustle of lizards and the spines of cactus, against whatever shapes lay in the darkness and whatever moved in the silence. Then Billy Bigelow and Dusty came in talking about the day. Only the sound of voices and the smell of chili seemed warm and real.

UNCLE LAZARUS

The fog had come in on something other than little cat feet, damp and impenetrable, and Mason Chalmers insisted that Kitty Bean let him off at the other side of the bridge that led down into Prospect Landing. He could get up the hill to his house on his own. Save her a trip over the winding dirt road and then having to back out of his narrow driveway. As it was, she'd be some little time making her way back to the camp she had rented. Who knew when the fog would lift? He wished he could offer her a place to spend the night, but his house was emphatically occupied. "Afraid to be seen in my company," she teased him.

If anything, he was afraid to be seen in his own, things having broken free from their moorings, its not yet being clear where they might settle. Everything seemed tentative, up for grabs. But he was in better spirits than he had been for months, thanks to her.

He leaned over, placed his hands on her shoulders, drew her toward him, and allowed the kiss to become an occasion in itself. "I'll be up next weekend," he said.

She put a finger up to his lips. "Best to make no plans."

"No," he agreed, "it's a poor idea. But . . ."

"You'll see me when you need to," she said. "And who knows, I may go off on one of my wanderings."

The years had not taken away her liveliness, her pride or determination. Her green eyes held their depth and sparkle above the lines in her face—she was still a beauty, her red hair a halo of fire around her face. And she was as maddeningly unpredictable as ever. "But you'll come back?"

"Of course I will. Haven't I always?"

"There have been some mighty long gaps in your appearances." The thought of her going off once again left him hollow.

"We came together long ago, and maybe there's something yet to be plucked from the future. It's still ripening, you know. Meanwhile you've got work to do."

Was she putting him to some sort of test?—it was quite like her.

"Do be careful, Mason—let me give you warning. That situation of yours has an ugly turn to it. Family or no, those folks are not on your side. I never did catch the scent of benevolence in Emma. Nor her kids, except for Nancy—poor thing. At least she had the sense to clear out."

"I think you've guessed it," he said. "Leaves you with a hell of a lonely feeling."

This time she leaned forward, put her arms around him, and as they kissed he was taken up more forcefully than ever into what he'd always felt for Kitty Bean. "It's been a great moment, Kitty," he said, when he'd caught his breath. "One for the annals of time. There aren't all that many."

"Your time and my time anyway." Her lilting laugh tripped down his spine like an arpeggio. She started up the motor, and he reluctantly got out of the car. He turned to watch her go with no thought of moving until the last suggestion of her truck lights had dimmed into the fog.

It wasn't all that late, only a little past sunset, but it was dark already. Light trapped by fog. *Brouillard*—he liked the word that had lingered from his college French, perhaps for just the right occasion. He had seen fogs plenty, but this one made him seem afloat as well, to put in a special call for clarity. The harbor was pretty well socked in, but for one thin veil trailing toward the hill; nothing to suggest, though, that the fog would lift anytime soon. He stood in its midst trying to get his bearings.

He walked over the bridge toward the store where his sister, Emma, sold gas and night crawlers and boating supplies, soft drinks, and groceries. His first thought was to walk on past—seeing her would only put a damper on his spirits. The years had settled them into a series of enforced pleasantries, a cover for a distrust he acknowledged but didn't like to dwell on. He would never have told her about Kitty or anything that mattered to him. But he was in need of a few things to tide him over—a loaf of bread, a jar of peanut butter, a can of coffee, and a little cream to put in it. He'd have a cup of coffee with her, just to delay going home. No doubt his niece and nephew had cleaned out the pantry and refrigerator by now, as they'd been in the habit of doing all that long summer. Whatever else had occurred during his absence he didn't care to speculate about.

He had no one to blame but himself. He'd been hit during a vulnerable moment, not long after Hannah died—left there in an empty house with only his cat, Samson, and Charlie to come in to help him keep the place fixed up. Charlie did his shopping and was creditable with a hammer and nails, but not much good with housekeeping. There was cat hair over all the furniture and a century of dust—or so it seemed. The house smelled of neglect. "You can't go on living like that," Emma scolded him. "The place'll go to wrack and ruin. And there's your health to think about. That Charlie is about as helpful as a crutch."

Then there was the problem with the well. First he got sick from what the doctor decided was food poisoning. Nothing he had eaten, he was convinced of that. Luckily it occurred to him to have his well-water tested. Full of E. coli bacteria, it turned out, after having been good pure water for thirty years. The only conceivable source was Herb Watkins's goats on the land just above him. But Herb stoutly denied his goats had anything to do with it. They'd been neighbors for a dozen years, the goats having come into the picture some months before. Mason's alternatives were a lawsuit or a new well. He chose the well as a matter of economy. It might cost him four thousand dollars, but a lawyer's fees, the pressure on his nerves, and bad blood on his borders were not worth the price.

His sister took issue with him, though it was none of her

affair. But she had raised him and had returned to her old habit of cor recting his life and issuing dire warnings. "You let him get away with that? You'll put yourself out of house and home if you don't watch out. You need someone to handle your affairs."

It was clear what she had in mind. Her daughter, Marlene, and Vernon, her son-in-law, had presented Mason with an offer to buy his house—with the proviso that he would continue to live there. Thereby keeping it in the family, keeping alive all the memories of Marlene's visits there when she was young. They'd be on hand to help take care of the place. He wasn't entirely con-vinced. He could smell something of motive, and very likely Emma was behind it—trying to do something for the younger generation, getting her ducks in a row. Her older daughter had come to grief, though of exactly what kind Emma refused to re-veal. Marlene and Vernon were the objects of her anxious care. If *he* agreed, they'd have something after he was gone: his land was getting more and more valuable all the time. Their offer, he thought, was on the skimpy side.

He knew he was going to have to make some decision about his house; sheer inertia had kept him from making a final will. He resisted any idea of selling the property and moving to an apart-ment; he'd lived in the house for over thirty years and was fully determined to die there. It was the outer casing of his personal-ity, of the life he'd lived within its walls. The old farmhouse he'd bought and redone had space and character. The kitchen with its pine cabinets and tongue-in-groove pine floors full of light. The sunporch where they'd taken their meals and watched the light dim behind the old barn. And the garden. Outside he'd plant-ed sweet peas of varied colors, and Hannah had her roses. He thought of all the auctions he and Hannah had gone to, looking for furniture with good wood, pieces they had prized over any-thing they could have bought new. And his study with its shelves of books, mostly history and biography, along with Shakespeare and a set of the Great Books—he'd always been a reader—his computer, and on the walls a couple of landscapes his mother had painted with a delicate touch and a certificate from the community commending him for his volunteer work.

If he sold the house to his niece, he'd have a little extra cash. He could pay off the debts that had come with Hannah's illness and his own time in the hospital and have something left over to leave to Charlie, who'd been with him for the past fifteen years. He said he'd consider it.

Apparently that was enough to convince Marlene and Vernon to come up from Augusta that summer, ostensibly to visit and to help him get back on his feet, but it became clear they had no intention of leaving. They moved in on him and took charge, as though they owned the place already.

They were hardly in the doorway when they told Charlie he was no longer needed. No use keeping him on, simpleminded as he was, unable to follow instructions unless you repeated them three or four times and supervised his every move.

"But it's his job," Mason insisted. "He's been with me ever since he hurt his back up at the mill." He'd put his foot down, but behind his back, they made Charlie's life so miserable, Charlie had left on his own. "You'll save twelve thousand dollars a year," Emma told him sagely. He was furious, not simply that they'd taken advantage of his weakness, but that he'd slipped into a cer tain lack of nerve.

As he drew closer, he saw a car sitting in front of the store, with Emma outside filling up the gas tank; she stood talking to the driver as he was counting out the bills. She knew everyone for miles around and pumped her regulars for gossip as they bought groceries and parts and fishing tackle and bait. Mason's brother-in law, Homer, a taciturn man and exacting mechanic, serviced their boats and trucks. The two of them had put by a tidy sum at one point but had lost considerably in the stock market.

"Well, Norman, you drive careful here in this fog," Emma said. There was a little conversation between them.

"No," Emma said. "After Marlene reported him missing, they had half the state out looking for him. Well, you heard the commotion. Helicopters flying over. Dogs tracking through the woods. Homer was gone for three days dragging the bay, along with the others-left me with all the work. He's dead tired. And I'm dead tired, let me tell you. All that labor for nothing."

The driver must have sympathized. Mason drew closer.

'I hate to say it, but . . . I'm sure he took his own life." There was a catch in her voice. "Nothing to live for after Hannah passed. Didn't leave a note or anything . . . That's right—the memorial's coming up the encl of the week."

He felt as though someone had landed a punch in the gut. He'd gone off without telling anybody where he was headed. Marlene and Vernon didn't have to know his every move—they weren't his keepers. It was a piece of resentment on his part. He hadn't figured they'd put him in his grave while he was gone.

He waited till she had a chance to put the bills in the cash drawer, glanced in to see that she was alone, and stepped inside. She had sat down on a stool behind the counter and opened the newspaper, perhaps to see what they were saying about him.

When she looked up and saw him, her normally impassive face—eyes that didn't miss a trick—was fixed in something moepowerful than dismay. She stood up jerkily, pressed her hand to her mouth, and gave a half-suppressed cry.

"I know why you've come haunting," she said in a tight voice. "They couldn't find your body, and you don't have the peace of the grave. Oh, Mason," she said, "that it should come to this." She held out a hand as though to stop his further advance. "We all understand how sometimes you can't go on. Just tell us where the body is," she said, "and we'll bury you right and proper. And where you've put the will."

He was himself astonished, even beyond hearing the news of his own death. It was his ghost she was seeing, even as he stood there in his Red Sox cap, his blue chambray L. L. Bean shirt and tan slacks, and Rockport walkers, vigorous and substantial, though his beard could have done with a little trimming. She was of too practical a mind—his will, eh?—he'd have thought, to let in the supernatural with the first whiff of the untoward, but she used to scare him with tales of ghosts and hauntings when he was a boy, maybe believed in them. Or else had wanted to induce the right sort of behavior on his part—he never knew. Perhaps she had planted him so securely in the other world, had so much now invested in his demise, she couldn't draw back.

He could have held up his arm with its good solid flesh and type O blood and invited her to give it a pinch, but for some reason he wasn't ready to undeceive her. The fog perhaps—must have put him in the mood.

He opted for a profound silence. *He* could hear the hum of the fluorescent lights on the ceiling and in the refrigerators. "Death is a hard thing, Emma," he said finally in a husky whisper, "when you *haven't* run out of things to live for."

She was silent as well, having to reconstruct his fate. "What happened to you, Mason?" she said, with a hint of desperation. "We searched everywhere."

"I went fishing."

"Fishing? Why, you haven't been fishing for over a year, not since . . ."

"Fortunately I got out of the slough of despond. Ray Thompson came along. You don't know Ray—a regular cut-up when he was young. Sold me a boat once that I swear had the inclination of a horse forever pulling toward the stable. And we've drunk many a beer together. Great fisherman. I can remember a time. Though the power of invention could have taken him by a longer route, he let it go. "He'd rented a camp up on Matawamkeag and came down after me. Hadn't seen one another in I don't how long. Just came and collected me and took me off in his truck.

"'Mason,' he said, 'let's see what we can do. This is just the lake for white perch—and you know as well as I do they're the best eating of all.'"

"You went that far?" She was putting things together. "So that's why your truck's right here-parked in front of the house. And no

116

note or anything about where you'd gone. We thought . . ."

Yes, I know what you thought. He watched her as she made an effort to work out the perplexity of things. He tried to make a space for contrition—he hadn't meant to give anyone trouble over him, but things had gone beyond him, and he was being carried forward in the momentum. It was no longer possible to continue what he'd been experiencing lately—an odd detachment from his own life.

The only help he managed to give her was to extend the plausibility of his fiction.

"Only, once I got fishing, the old appetite just came back. Ray had some business up in Houlton, so I got up early that last morning and went out on my own. I was out there in the middle of the lake when a line squall came up—a real doozy. Tried to get back before it struck, but it hit that boat and turned it around like a leaf, and the waves kicked up and suddenly I was swept out into the lake."

"Didn't you have a life jacket?"

"It got so hot before that squall came up, I took it off. Never figured anything like that would happen. Had it lying there right in front of me."

She stared at him, unblinking, but whether she'd swallowed the tale was unclear. The phone rang, and they both gave a start. When she turned away to answer it, he took the opportunity to slip away. He'd floated in the front door, so to speak, and caught her unaware, and it seemed a good moment to drift out again, disappear.

He counted on her to work things out afterward, figure he'd been playing her like a fish. Right now she was too rattled to think straight. Moments later he could hear her calling after him, but the fog was against her. For good measure he ducked into the trees and stood there, fueling another emphatic silence. *I am a figment of my own imagination,* he thought.

"So tell me about your life," Kitty Bean said to him. They'd taken the motorboat out on the lake over to a spot near the

117

far shore that, Kitty said, was promising for white perch. It was warm and sunny, a fine day in August, moving toward September. You could tell that things were winding down, the leaves of the trees hav ing grown rusty, as though they'd done their duty for the year. A few branches of the maples were going red in the swamps. But the goldenrod, all different species with their various heads and shapes, and the other late summer flowers-asters and sunflowers were still offering their vigor. And he had cause for celebration because Kitty Bean had come back once more, come for him, and they were sitting together there on the water, with a picnic basket of food she'd put together, thick meat sandwiches and potato salad, dill pickles, chocolate-chip cookies, and a thermos of lemonade.

He was back in another place and time—past his domestic troubles, past all thought of politics and war and the drift of the country, past the need to sort through the fictions that daily confronted him in the newspapers and on television and brought him to anger and cynicism. Small comfort that Hamlet had had a similar problem. But now there were just the two of them sitting there with most of their lives behind them, but still holding the vital thread of what had brought them together after all their separations. She had come for him, just come out of the morning in her truck and said, "Mason, here I am——I've come to spirit you away." And what could be better, out there on the lake with a fishing pole in his hand and Kitty sitting across from him.

He could reach all the way back to origins: *Kitty Bean, Kitty Bean.* His cousin's name had reverberated in his head with the rhythm of promise and delight, like a sky full of colored balloons. In kindergarten he'cl spun himself around with the rhythm of her name, and she, too, had spun around and around, the two of them breathless and giddy out there on the playground. Until, at the center of the whirling, a flame shot up and engulfed him heart and senses, liver and lights. He'd turned about in that flame through all his childhood and youth, even when her face had grown beyond his remembrance of her. Through the years that turned, it was the flame of his longing.

His first experience of loss came when he was six and his aunt and uncle moved off to New Mexico, taking Kitty with them. "Kitty's your cousin," his mother said. "You'll have to find another girlfriend." But then there was the tentative rediscovery of each other the summer his aunt and uncle came back east for an extended visit. The two of them were inseparable, hunting frogs together and fishing off the end of the dock. He'd given her his pocketknife, he reminded her. "Still have it," she told him.

"Then, when I came out to New Mexico that summer to help your folks with the orchard, they treated me like a member of the family." A feeling he'd never had with his father, or Emma, seven years older than he, who took over the household when his mother died. His aunt made his bed and washed his clothes and plied him with food, and his uncle taught him to ride a horse and let him drive his truck.

"Well, you were."

"The thing I chiefly remember," he said, "when I had the words to tell myself, was that suddenly I knew what love was. It was a discovery. My head was all full of you, but it was in the air, and I'd got hold of some of it—people treating one another not just like they mattered, but as though they could *see* you, see who you were and actually loved *that*. Maybe I'd never have known how it could bedone."

She smiled. "My mother said she thought you were love-starved and undernourished as well. 'That tight-fisted brother of mine—I never could find much sugar in the bucket,' that's what she said." He laughed. "Maybe that's why she kept trying to feed me." When they sat down to breakfast, the food was spread before him like a feast—eggs and pancakes, bacon and sweet rolls. Though it was Kitty he wanted to look at, his Aunt Mary also took his notice as he watched the way she prepared a meal, the way she handled every vegetable and piece of fruit—as though a single lettuce leaf was something to be prized. And the way they were all gathered around the table, his uncle Clyde and the three girls and his aunt.

The smells that lingered in the air, a distillation.

"It wasn't just food," he said, taking up one of Kitty's sandwiches. "It was what you put into it, the feeling when you sat dovvn to eat it. More than what you put in the stomach." It was moments such as these—ports of entry, he liked to think of them—where you entered a certain space that belonged forever to your imagination. Among all the seething possibilities of things coming together and falling apart, you had a sudden hope of clarity about what mattered. And, whatever happiness he'd had in his life, it was owing to those moments that he carried with him that served as a kind of paradigm for what he tried to create for himself.

"Too bad we didn't get married," he said to her.

"With two families beating on us about the idiot children we'd produce," she said, "there'd have been hell to pay."

He'd written Kitty love letters all the time he was in the army, but he'd never gotten any response. Kitty told him later that she'd never received the letters.

"We didn't have to have children," he said.

He had a bite on his line and tried to set the hook. "Got away," he said. He baited the hook again.

She shrugged. "I didn't think about that at the time. As it was, all I could do was go my own way, beat my head against stone walls. Not that I got all that far—probably we'd have ruined one another. You had a good long marriage, a place in the community," she offered. "Nothing to sneer at. I've been a rolling stone."

Indeed he'd loved his wife, though he'd have said now there was something left over that he'd never found a place for except in his imagination. Ironically, they had been childless. Meanwhile Kitty had had five husbands, owing to, he thought, no one being able to meet her match. Very likely she'd have been too much woman for him as well. Most likely she'd come into the world with a certain elevation of spirit and hadn't settled for anything less.

"When you married that first time, I was wild with jealousy."

That was jealousy but the flame turned green?

"Gus?" she said. "I gave him a hard time. He probably had reason to be jealous of you."

And what would he find now when he came back home, hardly his own anymore? Not simply occupied—usurped. Very likely Marlene would be working on the afghan she was copying out of some women's magazine. And Vernon would be planted in front of the TV, where he spent most of his time when he wasn't writing the Westerns that were going to make him rich, if not famous. He'd never been West, though he read Westerns by the dozen and took his landscapes from the pictures he saw in *Arizona Highways* he thumbed through in the library. Nor did he know anything of the habits of horses or cattle, or, Mason concluded, of men and women.

Meanwhile he palmed off his badly typed efforts to anyone who'd read them—maintaining they were at least as good as anything on the shelf in the Rite-Aid. Mason had been a captive audience. These were narratives filled with lawlessness and violence—hold ups, cattle-rustling, train robberies, shootings, hangings, and gen era mayhem. "You might throw in a little sex," Mason suggested at one point, "just for the sake of variety. It's what people like to read about." Vernon worried over the subject for a while then whipped a sheet out of the typewriter to show him. Mason was struck that he'd managed to do the job in a single sentence: "And then Nat Darby entered the saloon, took one of the girls upstairs and had his way with her. 'I needed that,' he said."

During these labors there were nearly three hundred pounds of him to keep stoked up. Mason did the cooking. That summer with Kitty had permanently influenced his ideas about food. During those years she was in charge, Emma had been able to put food on the table, mostly things she got out of a can. She could fry an egg and do up potatoes and macaroni and cheese, and she passed that knowledge on to him when she ran off to marry Homer. His father, captain of a ferryboat that went over to Saint John, was gone most of the time, and Mason fended for himself. Sometimes when he was home, they went out to eat. His father would go into the restaurant, leaving him to wait outside in the car. When he'd finished his meal, he'd bring Mason a hamburger. Once, bored with waiting, he got out of the car and went up to the window to look inside. His father was sitting practically next to the window, a plate in front of him with a steak and potatoes and all the trimmings. He ducked down quickly.

Once he learned what food could be, he decided to learn how to cook and had his Aunt Mary show him all her recipes. He carried home this new knowledge; and, during the time he was in college on a scholarship, he earned his spending money weekends as the cook in a small cafe. After his marriage he did his share of the cooking.

Usually he started the day with baking biscuits for breakfast, and at least twice a week he baked bread. Much better than the store stuff. He made pound cake and oatmeal cookies and yeast rolls. He gave much of it up for church bazaars or sent it round to the neighbors. Friends he invited over for roast chicken and dressing and mashed potatoes and gravy and vegetables that weren't cooked to death. And his homemade strawberry ice cream was cause for celebration. His niece and nephew tucked in three square meals without the blink of an eye; at least Marlene helped him afterward with the dishes. But the way the two of them packed it away, going through his meatloaves and mashed potatoes, loaves of bread and plates of cookies, all the groceries and ingredients out of his own pocket—the way they sponged off him—had turned him cranky and sullen.

When he suggested to Vernon that they chip something in for all they'd consumed that summer, his niece was not pleased. Finally, after waiting a week, they handed him fifty dollars.

He walked along trying to imagine how he would arrange his appearance. If the TV was on, he could enter without their hearing him, just appear out of nowhere. Could they, too, take him for a ghost come back to his old haunts? Full of portent and not exactly friendly. By now Emma had very likely phoned them up. Would she have raised the question of how he'd managed to keep hold of that baseball cap in the middle of a squall? "I was sure it was his ghost—like to scared me half to death. Only now I'm wondering. But if he's not dead . . . can he really be alive?"

More than likely Samson would settle the argument. Mason was sure he'd jump down from where he'd been curled up in his favorite chair, or else come out from under it to rub up against his leg—a dead giveaway. The cat had missed him terribly when he'd been in the hospital, had been all over him when he came home. Since Vernon and Marlene's arrival he'd spent a good deal of time hiding under Mason's favorite armchair. They didn't like the cat. "Now what's going on here," he could hear Vernon saying. "Folks all stirred up thinking you're dead. Maybe you can fool my mother . . ."

He would spare them further ambiguity. He was now ready to emerge—solid, reanimated—out of the fog. "It's your Uncle Lazarus," he'd announce to them, "come back from the dead." And when they'd taken that in, "I have a message for you—you can pack up your stuff and clear out. Tonight you can spend with your mama. And come for the rest of your things tomorrow. Charlie'll be here to help you." The idea had just struck him.

Charlie—of course, Charlie. Back as before, as he deserved to be—rescued from betrayal. If he would come back.

That meant that he had one more place to visit before he set foot in the house. It would take him an hour—more with the fog—to get to Charlie's trailer, where he lived with his wife, Jenny. Whereas Charlie was slow, Jenny was quick, and together they'd made a decent life. Their two grown daughters, both married, worked part-time waitressing in a restaurant up the coast.

Mason could take a little credit for him. He'd come upon

Charlie when he was a juvenile officer for the county. Charlie had run away from the foster home where he'd been placed, having been shunted from one relative to another, mostly neglected and very likely abused, and was living on the streets. What to do with him. The kid was sixteen and on the verge of getting into real trouble. Mason did what he frequently did with the kids he worked with—he took him fishing, taught him to fish. He'd found that out about some of those who came his way—if they took to fishing and enjoyed the companionship, they could get a glimpse of something beyond what they knew. He saw to it the boy got through high school—he wasn't the brightest, but he could get that far. And he was willing to work. He earned some real money working for the paper mill in Brewer, till he hurt his back. Then Mason took him on. Charlie needed work, and Mason needed somebody to help him keep the place up.

As Mason approached, Charlie's dog, a combination golden retriever and Newfoundland, made such a racket that through the window he could see Charlie get up from his armchair, slowly because of his arthritis, and move toward the door to see about the ruckus. Mason waited for him to open it. "What's got into you, dog?" Charlie yelled out into the fog.

"Hello there, Charlie," Mason said, stepping in close, while Charlie quieted the dog. "We haven't seen each other for a while."

Stunned, Charlie stared at him for a moment, as he stood there in the fog, then came hurtling down the steps and threw his arms around him. "I knew you weren't dead, Mr. Chalmers. I told it to Jenny. I said, 'I don't care what anybody says. He'll *be* back.'"

A big man, Charlie, and for a moment it seemed to Mason he'd be swept off the ground, what with him and the dog leaping up.

"Well, it's a good thing I'm here," Mason said, when they'd got their footing and he'd caught his breath, "seeing the state I left things in. I don't need to draw you a map."

Charlie gave a little self-conscious laugh.

"Come over to the house tomorrow," Mason said, "that is, if you're willing-after all this nonsense."

Jenny, who was standing in the doorway looking over the scene, didn't wait for his response. "Of course he'll come," she said. "He's been moping around here all summer. I'll be glad to *get* rid of him."

"Make it about nine," Mason said. "We'll have a cup of coffee—you and *me* with no interference—and I'll make you a list of what needs doing."

"You want me to pick up some doughnuts on the way?" Charlie asked. "I mean, if you don't have anything on hand."

"I'd count it lucky if there was a sack with crumbs in it. Chocolate icing on mine." He couldn't remember when he'd last made doughnuts; maybe he'd get out the recipe one of these days.

He'd be busy for a while. *He'd* have to send Charley for groceries before he could do any cooking. Meanwhile he'd throw open every window, air out the whole place. Change the sheets. Remove all trace of recent occupancy. He'd see if Mrs. Gresham would come in to do some cleaning, or one of the other church ladies. He had an accumulation in the closets and basement, stuff that had piled up over the years. No point in saving it. Some of Hannah's clothes he could give to the church for its rummage sale. And now that he was free to live, he'd make an appointment with Collins, the lawyer, to make out his will. His house would be his own, and when the time came, he'd be leaving it in good hands.

THE INK FEATHER

From inside, their voices rose, interlocked in quarrel, Adrian shouting as he always did, Mama protesting in her ragged way. She's fighting back, Willa told her dolls, Clarise and Isabelle, without conviction, as she sat on the swing in the little enclosed porch, where she had been taking out their appendixes. She had cut their sides open, taken out something that looked like a chicken heart, and sewed them up again. The hard-edged words of her brother's anger made her think of stones a mean boy once had thrown at her, and she could see her mother holding up her hands as though to fend them off, trying to make her voice into a wall. But it wasn't strong enough—there were breaks. The words were arrows that hit and stuck. And sometimes the voice began to fall away and die, barely able to make it into words—watery syllables. Then Mama would gather her forces, and the two of them would be at it again.

Clarise and Isabelle sat with painted smiles as though their operation had put them beyond the cares of the world. And Willa forgot them. Her ears had grown in the direction of the quarrel.

"Can't you at least try to be a human being? Surely you can find something better to do than watch soap operas and eat junk. The house is a mess."

"You weren't supposed to come home till Thursday," Mama protested. "You don't know what it's like to suffer-the agony in my back, and my hip."

"The same old excuses."

Adrian was scolding Mama as he always did for being so lazy and slow-moving and not keeping up the house. For every time she picked something up, she just turned around and set it down somewhere else, and nothing ever got put away. It meant nothing was ever lost, Mama said, though it seemed nothing was ever found either. "It's here somewhere," she would say, rummaging through this pile and that until something else distracted her. Meanwhile Adrian stood by, looking as though he wanted to tear the place apart and shake her till the stuffing came out. Willa could see it flying off in all directions.

Willa thought of how huge and soft Mama was, like a great pillow. "It's my thyroid," Mama always said, adding that when she was young she could touch the fingertips of her two hands around her waist. Now she was fifty-seven, terribly old, and Willa had been born late in her life. She hadn't believed she was pregnant till it was almost time for the baby to arrive. "It was just as much a shock to me as it was to everybody else," Mama was fond of saying. "It wasn't supposed to happen, right in the middle of the change. I hadn't had a period for nearly half a year. I thought it was a tumor."

"What's a tumor?" Willa had wanted to know.

"A growth, honey, and if you don't take it out, it kills you." But she'd been in there all the time, growing inside her mother's stomach, but not so anybody could tell—a secret, just growing. If she'd been a tumor, she wouldn't have come out and been herself at all. And how strange that would have been—not to be in the world, but maybe even stranger to have been a tumor and grown till Mama died. She was glad she had made the right choice.

Only she wasn't sure. Maybe she hadn't done the right thing to come into the world. Even Mama seemed to be of two minds: sometimes she was pleased about it and some times she wasn't. When she was pleased, she'd say:

"Just think of having a baby at that age—when I ought to be a grandmother. There's life in the old girl yet." And she'd laugh.

But Adrian was never amused. "You're obscene," he would say.

"How dare you? You came from the same place. But then you don't understand anything. You'll be all right when you get married, if you ever do. Maybe if you had a little fun yourself, you wouldn't be such a killjoy. Ah, if Frank had only lived . . ."

"All I need is a woman," Adrian had said sarcastically. "As though things aren't bad enough with the two of you around. At least Adam and Eve did something original," he said, pleased with his own wit. "God knows she made everybody suffer for it."

"And you're above it all. Think you're too good to be human. And what would you be, pray tell. Just because you've been to college . . . And what has it done for you except give you a better vocabulary for your nastiness?"

"Maybe if you kept your eye on something besides that idiot box you'd learn a thing or two," Adrian said over and over. And now he was saying what he always said: "But then you never did have a grain of sense."

Willa wanted to get up and go away, outside and down the alley to see Mary Anne. But it was winter outside and gray clouds hung over the whole world. And she was forbidden to go down the alley: she might stray off and get lost. The devil lived below the ground down in the alley, and if he saw you, he would come up and beat you with his stick. That was what Mama told her once when she'd wandered off. And once a man had been found in the alley beaten up so badly there was barely life in his body. He didn't know what had happened to him. But Willa knew that the devil had done it. Even so she liked to walk down the alley along the backyards of people's houses, though she was afraid the devil might get her.

Once back when she could barely remember, she had wandered off into an old stable. It smelled of hay and horses, a strong sweet smell of earth, though it was empty and the boards were broken in. And there she'd seen the black-and-white striped animal. She'd followed it out through the broken door saying "Kitty, here kitty." But it had walked slowly away from her and disappeared.

She'd been punished when she came home: no one knew where she'd gone.

"You were just lucky," Adrian said, when she told about the animal. "If you'd been hit by that skunk, you'd have had to sleep outside for the rest of your life."

128

And they marveled that the skunk had not sprayed her.

For a long time after that, she was good and didn't wander off and tried to be neat and tidy and to be a help to Mama, who couldn't move fast and was always complaining about her back and legs. But, no matter what she did, she had the secret knowing that the eye that looked upon her turned away in disgust. For it inevitably found her picking her nose or biting her nails or wiping her mouth on her sleeve or drop ping bits of food onto the carpet. One night Mama turned red and scolded her till the tears came for what she was doing under the covers.

Then one day it happened without her even thinking. It was summer and she was in the yard with nothing to do. She started to chase a swallowtail that flitted just beyond her in a dance of pause and flight each time she tried to sneak up on it. When she looked around again, she couldn't see her house. Then she saw a little girl watching her. She had blonde hair that caught the light when it moved and pale blue eyes, and she was thin and could run fast. Her name was Mary Anne, and she lived near where the houses ended and the fields opened up and the trees stood against the sky.

That day they had rescued the rabbit. They had seen it, both at the same instant, being carried off by a black tomcat with a white nose and a torn ear and two yellow eyes that burned his seeing into whatever he looked at. He was advancing down the alley when they saw him with the bit of fur in his jaws. He gave them a quick look, about to dodge away with his prize. In that instant Willa saw that it was a rabbit, just a baby, and before she thought she made a rush at the cat. And the little girl, too, came running out of her yard. The cat ran under a bush, and they trapped him there against a wall. They tried to make him let go, while he clawed at them and growled and tried to sink his teeth deeper into the little rabbit. At last the cat leapt away with a yowl and left them with his victim.

The little girl held the creature in her hand, stroking its fur, while Willa threw a handful of pebbles after the cat to scare it off.

"You're safe now, little rabbit," she crooned. "We saved you."

But it lay still in her hand.

"Is it dead?" Willa asked, anxiously, breathlessly. It would be terrible if it were dead.

"No," said the little girl. "I can feel its heart. Maybe it's just frightened." She set it down on the ground and stepped back Willa held her breath, watching. For a long moment the rabbit didn't move. Then suddenly it was leaping away. "Be more careful next time, little thing," the girl said. And then to Willa: "Come and play. I'll tell you a dream I had." How she escaped a whipping when she got home was a miracle to her. But Mama hadn't missed her, and Adrian was deep in his study with the door closed. She had come home with such dread her fear sat like a great stone on her chest. She had not been found out, but what would happen if she got away with it? She was pulled between wanting to tell and get it over with and dreading what Adrian would say or do if she confessed. She stood for a long time in front of the door to his study wanting to knock. Once she got her hand almost to the door.

She even felt the stirring of an old curiosity. Only once had she ever been inside. Adrian never allowed anyone to enter his study, not even Mama, for she might break something valuable when she dusted or mess up his papers. But sometimes when he sat at his desk he lef t the door open, and Willa could look inside if she was careful not to make any noise. Otherwise he would roar "Can't you see that I'm working? Go out and play, will you?"

The walls were covered with shelves of books that looked very old, with gold letters on the backs. And they had an old smell about them. Adrian managed a shop in which he sold them and other things as well—all old things. For some people wanted them more than they wanted new things and paid a lot of money for them. Sometimes he traveled to foreign lands and came back with things so rare and precious that hardly anyone could afford to buy them. Once in a while he would come home in great spirits saying that a certain collector had bought the such-and-such. "He has millions, of course. A mere trifle for him." When Willa tried to imagine such a human being, she thought of money stacked up to the ceiling.

There were figures on the shelves, carved of ivory and ebony wood, Adrian had told her. He had a great desk of dark wood where he sat and wrote letters and did arithmetic with big numbers. Under his chair was a white sheepskin rug. A large green blotter lay across the desk where Adrian wrote, always with an old-fashioned ink pen, in lines straight across the page or in long columns down it. She had watched him that one time and thought how neat and beautiful his writing was. She wished she could write like that instead of in the big stumpy, crooked letters that came out of her pencil and slanted down the page.

She had come home from school with her report card that one time, and he had called her in so that he could look at it. She had gotten C's in arithmetic and reading, so that he was neither pleased nor displeased. And when he had looked at the card, he hadn't told her right then to go out and play. She had remained standing on the rug, white and fleecy beneath her feet, and watched him dip his pen into the crystal inkwell with the little brass top and write as though he were writing directions for the world. She had looked around at the shelves with their carved figures that could have been people or animals, she wasn't sure. Quite without thinking, she had pointed to one and said "What's that?" And Adrian had taken down an ivory figure, a dancing lady with flowers at her feet. She mustn't touch, and she held her breath before the delicate object lest she break it simply by breathing on it. It looked very old. Then she had gone out before Adrian told her to go. And her heart had given a little leap because he hadn't mentioned anything she had done wrong.

Now it was as though Mama were the child who must be scolded because she had done something wrong. Mama was cry-ing. Willa could hear Adrian's voice descending like a club.

"Your own mother," Mama wept. "How can you treat me like this?"

"It's just what you deserve. If you weren't so stupid . . ." Willa wanted to take Mama in her arms and rock her and sing to her as she sang to her dolls. She went to the door and opened it.

"What do you want?" Adrian demanded, bashing around toward her. "What have you been up to?"

But she didn't dare say anything and she didn't move. "The world's turned upside down," Mama moaned, "children raising their voices to their parents, young against the old. The sky will rain blood." As she moaned, she rocked back and forth. "The cruelty of your own flesh and blood. If only I had known . . ."

"Well, say something," Adrian said furiously as Willa hung in the doorway. "Don't just stand there like a lump."

"I want to go and play with Mary Anne," she blurted out before she knew what she was saying.

"What?" Adrian demanded. "Who is Mary Anne?"

Exposed, she had to tell the truth. "My friend. She lives down the alley," she said in a quick breath.

"Why, where'd you ever get that idea, child?" Mama said, looking at her, puzzled but not angry. She exchanged a glance with Adrian.

"She's making it all up," Adrian said. "No wonder she does so badly in school. She's always lost in a cloud."

"She is too my friend," Willa insisted. "She has a real father and mother."

"Which is more than I can claim," Adrian said, instead of asking her how she came to know Mary Anne.

Willa looked at Mama. She was big and fat, but she wasn't a tumor. She was just Mama.

"O Lord!" Mama said indignantly. "Which is worse—disrespect to the living or insulting the memory of the dead?"

"What was he when he was alive?" Adrian demanded.

"That's the insult. A cheap drunk—a common bricklayer, who couldn't even support his family."

"He did his best. The world beat him down."

"The sot."

"You're inhuman."

"And you're a mess."

Willa breathed a sigh of relief. They had forgotten about Mary Anne.

"You always took up for him. Sat back and let him go through money like water. I could have been somebody if I'd been given half a chance."

"You hold everything against me. Consider what I had to live through."

"You grovelled in it. You . . ." And his hand shot out as though he would grab her by the hair and tear it off the way Willa once had yanked the wig off her doll and left her bald.

"He did his best," Mama repeated inanely.

Willa couldn't remember her father, though she had two pictures of him in her head. When Mama talked about him, she saw a long-faced man with sad eyes and a puckered brow; but when her brother spoke, she turned away from two eyes like coals flashing fire and was stung by an evil-smelling breath.

"You live in the past," Mama said. "The dead past that can't be changed."

"And you can't see it," Adrian said. "You paint it up like a piece of calendar art."

Since they had forgotten about her, Willa went back on the porch to Clarise and Isabelle. She was going to give them another operation. She was going to take out their eyes and put them back in straight so they wouldn't be all cross-eyed and squinty.

For his vacation Adrian had gone back to the town where he'd been born, but he'd come home before it was time and was in a far worse temper than he'd been in before he left. "It's all your fault," he yelled at Mama. "I couldn't walk anywhere in that town without people pointing at me and turning away. They refused to speak a word to me. And all for being Frank Clayborne's son and having you for my mother. They couldn't forget. I couldn't go back and hold up my head—all because of you." And he then turned and flung himself into his study and even slammed the door.

Her arm around Willa, Mama wiped her eyes and shook her head. "There's not one word of truth in it," she said, "but he believes it like the gospel. Craziness—the stories he tells. He says I beat him every day when he was little—imagine! Says I put plates of food on the table but made him go hungry; says I rapped his knuckles with a ruler every time he reached for something to eat; claims I dressed him in rags; says I wanted to sell him to the gypsies that came through once; tells people he had to sneak off to go to school. To think I brought him into the world." She gave Willa a series of little light pats on the shoulder, but it was clear she wasn't thinking about her.

"He was different when he was little. We were poor then, and he did all kinds of things to help. He made crepe-paper flowers and sold them to the neighbors; raised pigeons and sold the squabs, and rabbits. When he was in high school, he wanted to be an actor. Used to stand with his face in the mirror practicing—bugging out his eyes, pulling down his mouth at the corners, stretching his grin from ear to ear—till his face was like a rubber mask and he could do anything with it. And I think he stretched it out of shape, till it wouldn't go back, till it twisted something inside him too." Willa tried to imagine the rubber mask, but now Adrian's face with the yellowed skin tight against his cheekbones was more like varnished wood, despite the pendulous lobes of his ears and the nose that ended in a little globular drop as though it were starting to melt. His face looked cracked like old wood, but when he was angry his eyes blazed up. And when he yawned he looked as though he could swallow her.

His teeth were very white and even.

"And yet," Mama went on, "strange things have happened to him. Said once he found a thousand dollars in the street. Said he was the escort of the Queen of Denmark when she came to visit in France; said a movie star fell in love with him just from seeing him across the room. Said he owned a manuscript of poems by a great Irish poet and that these were stolen. Said he escaped death from a crazy man who swore he'd kill him because he looked like his brother. And all these things are true. And now I ask you, what's the sense in any of it?"

Willa wanted to know whether he'd be any different if all his lies were true and all the true things were lies.

Mama thought for a long time. "He would be neither better nor worse. For he believes in his own lies. No," she said, "not meaner, nor smarter, nor kinder. Nor easier to tell when he'd be any of these."

For sometimes he came in with a swagger like a soldier, holding himself so that his chest seemed to lead him into the room, and his head could have been fastened to his body by an iron spike instead of a neck. And sometimes he surprised them by leaping in front of them, dancing round them in a circle and laughing at their shocked silence. And often he was railing and cursing because nothing was right in the world. And now and then he was friendly and polite and spoke in a voice like other people. But you could never count on him for anything, for if he was kind, he could turn mean, and if he was angry, he could suddenly crack a joke. "Now I ask you, what's the sense in any of it?" Mama said again. "Look at what's happened to me—look at this picture." She showed Willa a sepia snapshot of a young girl with ringlets around her head and a face like a morning glory. "Now would you say I was the same as she? And what's become of the thoughts in my head then? Gone . . . even when I try to remember. When I was little, I could run like the wind—and I thought if I flapped my arms I could fly. Now look at me." She tried to get up, heaving herself forward like a mountain looking for the faith to move it, then sinking back again. "Misery—there's a devil in the flesh, though nobody believes it any more."

"Are you going to sit there all day until you grow into that chair, or fix me something to eat?" Adrian said, as he reappeared from his study.

"You've put me in such a mood I don't care whether you eat or not," Mama said. "A lot you care for me . . . If you knew what

I suffered in these legs and back . . ."

"Rationalizations. You talk yourself into it." She looked at him. "I suffer."

"It's all in your head."

"Go away," Willa burst out suddenly.

"Don't you talk back to me," he said, advancing toward her with his hand raised.

She dodged behind Mama's chair.

"Let her be," Mama commanded. "She's only a child."

"This is the way you bring her up. What's she going to turn into, I ask you?"

"I've taught her to be a good child. To mind her manners and be clean and helpful—which is more than you do."

"You're not fit to be anybody's mother."

"O God—listen to him."

And they went on lashing each other, exposing each other's failings. As usual Willa moved away toward the door to go and take refuge with Clarise and Isabelle. Maybe she would cut out their tongues. She opened and closed the door quietly, putting the thickness of wood between herself and the voices inside. She had not been playing long when she heard a little light tap at the front door. Though it was fogged with moisture, she thought she recognized who it was and wiped away a circle with her hand. It was Mary Anne, and for a moment the two of them stood and made faces at one another, laughing soundlessly, for Willa had put her finger to her lips for silence. Then she opened the door without a sound and beckoned her friend inside. "Come out and play with me," Mary Anne whispered, under the cover of the voices that clashed within.

Willa reached for her coat from the coat tree and put on her boots. "Bet it's cold out," she said. The heat inside the enclosed porch had made the windows completely fogged, so that she could not see out.

"But the snow's all sparkly and there are icicles to eat." And Willa remembered how she had heard one crack and fall into

136

the snow like a dagger. Suppose I pick it up, she thought, and smash the sun right in the eye.

Quietly they left the porch and stepped out into the snow. A little white curly-haired dog rejoiced when they appeared and tore off as fast as it could go. "Come on," cried Mary Anne, as she began to chase after the dog, taking great strides through the snow. Willa tried to follow, though she had to be the first to stop, quite out of breath. They walked along toward the open fields, where the evergreens were cut out against the snow. The snow was a field of diamonds. Willa jumped up and down.

"Listen, and I'll tell you what I did yesterday," said Mary Anne. "I went out to play in the snow all by myself. The grown-ups were all inside by the fire and didn't want to come out. But I came out with Tina, and we ran and ran till we were all out of breath. I chased her and she chased me. Then we began walking, and suddenly we came to a place where the snow just stopped and it was all green grass. Everywhere you looked there were peach trees all covered with peaches, yellow and ripe."

"I can see it," Willa said, for as Mary Anne told it she was there herself.

They made angels in the snow and built a snowman, and when Willa thought to look again, the sparkle was gone and the light was sinking. A crow flew overhead, cawing hoarsely, its shadow flickering across the snow. And she heard in it Adrian's voice.

She ran home then, fingers and toes now numb with cold. The cold outweighed her fear, though she knew what awaited her. But when she opened the door and went inside, the house announced its emptiness. The warm breath of heat made her skin tingle, and she heard the furnace making little clicking sounds. It was strange to be there alone in the house, just herself in the space between the walls. And she had a strong sense of Mama's presence and Adrian's as separate and distinct from her.

The door to the study was open, but with Adrian gone something had been taken away, as in a problem in subtraction. She went inside and stood by the desk, right where she had stood before. She knew she wasn't supposed to be there, not even to look, for even with Adrian's absence the room belonged to him and spoke his disapproval. She picked up his pen, lifted up the top of the inkwell and dipped it in. And while the room waited in forbidding silence, she made one tiny scratch on an envelope, then another.

She heard the door flung open.

"Where can she be—oh, where can she be?"

"Wait'll I get my hands on her. She won't sit down for a week."

"She's gone—she's gone."

Horrified, she stood rooted to the spot as though she grew there. Then something gave way, and it didn't matter. She swept her arm across the desk and knocked over the inkwell. The inkwell shot to the floor, making a great spray on the rug. It was a creation. It looked like a feather drawn by the ink. It should have been white, but it was dark, and instead of lifting in flight it sank into the fleece. But she liked it, it was hers, there on the ground. And with a certain dark exultation, she knew her secret: even if the devil found her, she'd sneak down the alley to look for Mary Anne.

SIRENS AND VOICES

After Herman Carmody and his wife, Bobbie, had made love with gratifying ardor and lain for a time in each other's arms, and he had fallen into a profound sleep, Bobbie lay staring into the darkness. Two dogs kept her awake with their barking, rather like a man and a woman quarreling: blasts of deep resounding bark, followed by a monotonous querulous yipping. Then the two intersected. Then one. Then the other. A car door slammed—probably Dee Dee Dishinger coming home from her date: Bobbie could hear loud hilarious goodnights. She remembered a rumor about the girl having been caught shoplifting a dress from one of the stores in the mall. She suspected it was true: the girl was cute—she ran with the country-club set. Her folks were poised on the thin edge of extravagance. The girl wanted nice things; Bobbie couldn't blame her.

Bobbie wanted something herself, but she had no idea what it was. Chocolate cake, she thought, trying to seize hold of an image of what had created her longing. No, lemon pie with meringue three inches high. No, not that either. What then?

When the noise subsided, the mindless chirr of insects took over, and the night went grinding on like her own invention. It was as though a gang of foreign invaders had taken over the territory of her mind and set up some tacky provisional government with endless factions warring for control. She remembered suddenly that Ricky had to have a cowboy hat for the school play.

Next to her came a whimper like a faint cry from a distance: Herman in his sleep. But he did not wake up, not even for the commotion down the street. First, a police siren came wailing ever closer till it ceased with a little burp right in the neighborhood. Then the ambulance.

Curious, grateful for any distraction from her hunger, Bob

bie slipped out of bed and went to the window. She couldn't see anything. She had to be content with speculation. Among the neighbors on this or the next block, it could have been accident, sickness, sudden death. But farther on, in the midst of a row of houses on the decline, in a derelict gray apartment house, it could have been a drunken brawl, a stabbing, or a domestic quarrel that included a gun.

She hung by the window, as though, simply by her waiting, the event would reveal itself to her. She thought of putting on her clothes and going down to the street, but it wouldn't look right if anybody she knew saw her. In the morning she'd find out from Ramona Tulloch, who knew everything worth knowing in the town, and who, if she didn't know herself, would find out from somebody who did.

She eased herself back into the four-poster bed and lay staring up at the canopy. The shadow beyond the foot of the bed was a bureau of burly walnut, and to the side, where she couldn't see it, stood a little dressing table that had made her cry out with delight when Herman brought it home from the auction. The house was quiet as she lay in her nest of shadows. Too quiet. Till shadow and quiet parted and she was struck by an idea. Of course, that's what they could do with the third floor. Ah! Herman: she put her mouth around the syllables. How she wanted to wake him. To tell him: she had discovered where they could put a jukebox. She had always wanted one.

"I don't know why we never thought of it," Bobbie said, as she poured herself a second cup of coffee. A bit ragged this morning. Had hardly been able to sleep once the idea had seized her.

The breakfast nook was a sunny, if nervous, little corner where the light kept dancing in and out, at times too much for her eyes. Herman, only half-awake himself, was trying to concentrate on what she was saying.

"All this time that third floor has just been sitting there," she said. "And do you know what?" Her enthusiasm swept over him, left him blinking. "We'll make it into a bar. Counters and stools on one side. A jukebox in the corner."

"A jukebox?" he said, looking up to where a great spider plant filled the window and, suddenly molten in the sun, sub sided into the light. "A jukebox?"

"It'll be *fun,*" she said. "Think when people come over—we can dance, really live it up. Our own private disco. And what about a player piano?"

She amazed him, she'd always amazed him—the things she could come up with. Even now when he thought there was not one more thing they could possibly do to the house. "But is there money?" he asked.

"Of course there's money," she said. "There's always money."

That too amazed him: he knew nothing about money. Bobbie always handled the finances: she counted out the cash, paid the bills, knew how much they had spent and for what; while he floated somewhere above the hard edges of facts, somewhere below the insistence of her desires, the whispers of currency in between.

"Then in the end wall," she went on, "a tank with tropical fish and plants—maybe the whole end wall."

The whole wall a fish tank: he was trying to imagine it. Just beyond him, from the cage in the corner, a great fluttering of green and blue wings, a squawking of budgerigars. A small touch of the exotic in the modern kitchen. And now for the fish kingdom.

"Are you listening?"

"Of course," he said, trying to clear away distractions. Was it his hearing, he wondered, or a certain sluggishness of mind that failed to keep up with the astonishing fertility of her imagination? Though he was an interior decorator, his mind had been as chaste as a monk's cell till Bobbie had gotten hold of it. Now it had come to resemble one of those huge auction barns, treasure piled next to trash, with hardly a space to walk through.

"I want all kinds," she insisted. "Angel fish and striped sergeant majors and piranhas and the little creatures that look like streetcars lit up at night."

"Would they get along?" he wondered.

"Of course. You just have to keep them fed."

He considered. What if you forgot sometimes, or if not all of them ate those unappetizing thin wafers he'd fed to gold fish as a small boy, but had each a special diet that included each other? Or suppose you forgot to feed them, and instead of the endless indifference of circling fins there was the awak ened eye of appetite?

"Don't you think it's a wonderful idea? Aren't you excited? And you know when I thought of it?"

"Where would we find a jukebox?" it occurred to him to ask. "In Florida when we go. There's bound to be one there. You know when I thought of it?"

A jukebox from Florida. "No—when?"

"Last night—after the police cars came."

"When was that? I didn't hear any police cars."

"No," she said. "You were asleep."

The gleaming new meat counter in Slater's Market was a feature designed to convince the customers that here were the best meats in town at the highest possible prices. Two women were standing in front of the counter, behind which Ellis Slater kept bobbing back and forth between the scales and the conversation, weighing out meat and trying to get things straight.

"Can you believe it?" Ramona Tulloch said. "Dead—just like that." She snapped her fingers. "I walk right by his place every day. Didn't occur to me I hadn't seen him since Tuesday. I'll take a pound of that ground round, Ellis."

"How strange," Bobbie Carmody said. "Last time I saw H. T. he was acting downright antisocial. Like he didn't want to talk to anybody. Herman's done a lot of worrying over him lately. He's going to take it hard."

"He the fellow that took the waitress home and held her for three hours and tried to rape her, only she escaped when he had to go to the toilet?"

"Of course not, Ellis—that was one of the teachers, and they fired him and he's left town for good."

"He's not the one that liked little boys, is he? Used to proposition them on the playground?"

"Whatever gave you that idea? H. T.'s the one the kids used to call 'Doc.' Was a counselor at the high school."

"Lived alone," Bobbie added, "in that little garage apartment on South Home."

"Sure, sure, I know who you mean now. Always came in and bought the same thing: two pork chops and a pint of coleslaw from the case. Always wanted to know if it was fresh."

"Is that today's liver?—give me a pound."

"Yeah, now I know," Ellis said, reaching for the pan of livers. "Doc. Good-looking fellow. Laughed a lot. Always alone except for the kids. You think he was—"

"All the kids loved him," Bobbie said. "Came around all the time to tell him their troubles."

"He once told me there'd been a great grief in his life, but he never would say what it was," Ramona Tulloch said.

"A man that old without a woman . . ." The butcher shook his head. "Now I don't call that natural."

"Remember how Eva Faye Brownley used to lie in wait for him as he walked home? Kept inviting him to dinner. Actually proposed to him."

"A sad case," Bobbie said. "Married to that brute for so long, then going to pieces when he died."

"Then there was the one that married the opera singer—can't think of her name—went off to California."

"Chased anything that wore pants."

Ellis laughed. He laid the package with the liver next to the others. "What did he die of anyway?"

"They don't know yet. Just found him dead—had been dead three or four days. They're waiting on the coroner's report."

"That's what comes of being alone. It ain't healthy," Ellis said. "I should have asked him to come to our church."

Bobbie was wondering if H. T.'s drinking had finally done him in. Herman had tried to talk some sense into him. "Her man and I were in high school with him," she said.

"I bet there's a woman in it somewhere," the butcher insisted. "See if I'm right."

On Valentine's Day, Bobbie remembered, all the girls pinned hearts on H. T.'s door. He used to joke about it. "See all my girls—they're in love with me."

As Herman turned down Home Street toward his place of business, he noticed an unusual activity, as of wasps or hornets moving in and out of their hive, and located the source and target of movement as the doorway of the little garage apartment where H. T. Morgan lived—Ole Doc, as the kids fondly called him. The coroner was coming down the steps in Herman's direction: Lyman Cleaver, a tall, hearty horse-faced man with tobacco-stained teeth. Along with being coroner, he ran the local funeral parlor, a brick building on the corner of Main and South, where he frequently stood in the doorway, thumbs looped in his vest, greeting people as they passed by—out of an inexhaustible sociability. He knew everybody, above ground and below.

"'Morning, Herman," he said. "You heard the news? Terrible thing. Friend of yours, wasn't he—H. T.?"

"Good God, what's happened?"

Cleaver shook his head, grimaced as if he might be genuinely puzzled. "Been dead for three days at least. Didn't show up at school. Didn't answer the phone or the door. Finally had to have the sheriff break in the door and there he was . . ."

"I can't believe it. What could have happened?"

The coroner, thumbs looped in his vest, leaning back, one knee slightly bent, was ready with an answer. "Looks to me like he electrocuted himself. The way he was laying across the bed, foot dangling next to a bunch of cords. That's the way I figure it."

"Why, that's terrible. Poor old H. T." He hardly knew what to say. He struck out blindly. "You don't suppose he got sick maybe had a heart attack?"

"Of course we can't tell anything till they run the lab reports," the coroner said. "And we can't rule out the possibility of foul play."

"But that's preposterous," Herman said. "Who'd want to kill H. T.?"

"You never can tell."

(Maybe. Maybe there's always someone around who'd like to knock you off. More likely, Herman thought, H. T. had staggered into the cords. Probably blind drunk. Could he have wanted it? A chilling thought. But the way H. T. was drinking lately you could almost believe . . . He tried to remember back to a time when things might have gone differently, when he might have turned him around. He'd tried hard enough. Like talking to the air. Everything he said H. T. treated like a joke, just shrugged it off. But it was all bluff—you could tell. Once he'd let down the facade: had ended an evening of drinking down at the Elks' Club by bursting into tears, had sat there weeping and hiccuping and shaking his head as though over some unfathomable and terrible fact. There was an embarrassed hush among the fellows at the bar. A couple of them came over, patted him on the back, tried to joke him out of it. Then they left him alone: crying drunk, that's all. It could happen. So they went back to their own drinking, and the hubbub rose around them again.)

"Is he really dead?" Herman asked incredulously.

"What do you think I said?" the coroner responded, looking at Herman as though he didn't have good sense. "Guess I know a dead man when I see one."

But that wasn't what he meant.

"Well, got to get back," the coroner said. "How come you never drop by the Elks any more? They got some great new flicks."

If he said they bored him, that he had a wife at home he

found far more interesting, they'd never believe him. "Don't have the time," he said.

The coroner clapped him on the shoulder. "You got to make time, old buddy. Gotta relax, enjoy. Don't take it too hard," he advised. "Can't let things get you down. Come on over tonight and I'll buy you a drink." The yellow teeth came forward in a grin to put off the doleful.

"Thanks—some other time," Herman said. My God, he thought, H. T.'s gone, and tried to imagine the world continuing without him.

At the same time that the *Evening Star Bulletin* was coming off the press with a picture of H. T. (Doc) Morgan smiling across the front page—deceased, cause of death as yet undetermined— Herman was ringing the doorbell at a home on the east side of town, in the Green addition. Doctor's house: game room, wine cellar, swimming pool, tennis courts. Dr. Bannister. Divorced and remarried. New wife wanted the house completely redecorated.

He hadn't wanted to come, but he made himself keep the appointment: unfair to impose your troubles on your customers.

The woman who answered the door and stood smiling, as though she herself were the climax of an extraordinary joke, looked familiar.

"Don't you recognize me, Herman?" she said. "You must have read about the wedding."

"Eloise Moaks!" he said, startled into memory. He never read the newspaper. If he'd heard her name, it hadn't registered. "What are you doing here? I thought you were a nun." "I was," she said. "Only now it's Eloise Bannister. But do come in. It's wonderful to see you again."

She was dressed as though a bridge club might be arriving any moment: gold earrings, gold necklace, many gold bracelets on her wrists, sending off little gleams and jangles as she stood in a white dress of a rough, yet clinging sentiment. The aura of her perfume rose evocatively around her.

146

"I know it's a shock," she said. "But suddenly it came to me it wasn't the lifestyle I wanted. Deep inside I had other aims and goals. Until I met Carleton I never really found myself."

(Found herself?—found herself a man—that was what he heard Bobbie saying with a derisive laugh. The wonder is she didn't find one in high school.)

"It was our work that brought us together," Eloise went on, "with those poor children in the home. Poor lost lambs. He was so lonely then, Carleton was—just lost, poor darling. He used to talk and talk—Leila never really understood him. One thing led to another and here we are." She opened her arms, making Herman a presentation of her new life. "But tell me about yourself."

There wasn't much to tell. He'd started off in cushions and drapes at Sears after turning down a chance in underwear, then worked his way up to carpets. After Bobbie's father had died and his share of the business was sold, Bobbie had set Herman up as an interior decorator.

"In high school I had the biggest crush on you," Eloise announced. "You wouldn't even look in my direction."

His face flushed.

"What did you ever see in Bobbie anyway?"

"She has nice teeth," he said, trying for escape. Something simple, even simpleminded.

"Nice what?"

"Nice teeth. I always admired her smile."

"Pooh," she said. She wasn't going to let him get away with it. "Is that why you married her?"

Her irony made him perspire. What a question! Why did anybody get married? You saw a doorway open and you thought Ah love—go for it! If you discovered reasons . . . it was afterwards.

"Silly me," she said. "It's all water under the bridge."

"Nice place you've got here," he said lamely.

"It will be," she said meaningfully, "when I get through with it. I want it all in white: white carpet, white furniture, white walls, white drapes. Just for a note of contrast I've thought of getting a

147

Siamese cat. But now that I think of it, an ocelot would be more dramatic."

"Definitely more dramatic," Herman said, as he reached into his jacket pocket for his glasses, took out his notebook.

"Oh, there's time for all that," she said. "But first how about a little drinkey-poo?"

Drinkey-poo? Had he heard right? "No I—"

"Come on now, don't be so stuffy. For old times' sake."

She went to the bar at the end of the living room and poured out two generous sloshes of scotch. "I take mine on the rocks," she said, handing him a glass. Perhaps it was a challenge.

He took a tentative sip, rather like a high-school girl trying out her first whiskey sour. He didn't like to drink during working hours—he had a low tolerance for alcohol. But it was good scotch and went smoothly down.

"Sit by me," she said, patting the spot beside her on the sofa. He sat down as if on command. "There—that's more relaxed, isn't it?"

It was better—only worse. Given a strong invitation by her perfume, something inside him began to waver and float. He didn't trust himself. He had the feeling she knew his susceptibilities.

"You know," she said, looking into his eyes in a way that unnerved him, "the years have done well by you. You look mature."

"Well I . . ." He shrugged. Words eluded him.

"Even distinguished," she said. "And I . . . don't I . . . don't you . . ."

She was waiting. "Mature," he said. "Very mature." She frowned: clearly he had disappointed her.

"You're lovely," he said. It was what she wanted to hear, but was it what he wanted to say? He had just enough presence of mind to say, "I think you should tell me what you want me to do."

"That's easy," she said, getting up immediately. "Come in here."

He stood up uncertainly.

"I want to start in the bedroom," she said. "With the interior."

The doorbell rang. They had come to measure for storm windows.

Precocious interruptus, Herman thought. Beads of sweat broke out on his forehead.

Since it was the end of the month, Bobbie had worked late that evening. After the two younger partners had taken over her father's advertising firm, she had stayed on as bookkeeper, working afternoons. Before she could begin supper, though, she had had to drop off Gloria, her daughter, to spend a night with a girlfriend, and buy a cowboy hat for Ricky. When Herman came home, he found Bobbie in the kitchen making spaghetti.

"I tell you," she said, "if I'd only known what I know now, things would sure be different. They made it sound like they were losing their shirts. I'm sure that lawyer did some fancy finagling. And I'll bet you Dempsey Stringfellow made it worth his while. Now they're making a mint. They think I don't know what the score is-that I'm too dumb to figure things out."

"But we're doing all right, aren't we?" Herman said mildly. For some reason he was remembering the way Stringfellow had looked at Bobbie during the festivities of the last office Christmas party. "Maybe you should quit," he said.

"Don't be silly. The point is, fair is fair."

"I still think you should quit," Herman said. "We can get by."

"It's been a day," she said, ignoring him, setting plates of spaghetti in front of them, then sitting down. "I suppose you heard the news."

"About H. T.? Lyman Cleaver told me. I still can't believe it." He laid down his fork.

"And to die like that—all alone."

"They think he might have electrocuted himself. And if he'd been drunk . . . senseless, senseless."

"You think that's what happened?"

149

"I don't know."

"Do you think he could have . . ." She looked at him and paused. It was in both their minds.

"I don't know. He was drinking like a fool. I haven't gone around there for weeks. I just couldn't stand it. Every time I went by, there he was, smashed out of his mind with a room full of kids pouring out their hearts. I wonder if that's why he drank."

"He was their god—they all came to him."

"Only maybe underneath . . ." He paused. Ole Doc. With a smile and a joke for everyone. Except that one night when he'd seen the curtain drawn back . . . He didn't want to think about it—how when you drew back the curtain and there was nothing left you could call rational . . .

"I don't know," Herman said. "Maybe it was just an accident." Did that make things any better?

"I always thought he had a mother complex," Bobbie said, "the way he ran from women. And he was a marshmallow."

Herman saw the fires of hell. Marshmallow? A blackened cinder.

"The world's a tough place. You got *to* be tough. Sometimes I just want *to* strike out where it would do the most good. Stringfellow, for instance. Seems like every time I turn around, he's looking over my shoulder."

"I wish you'd quit."

"I can't."

"Why not? We're doing all right, aren't we?"

"You know," she said, with sudden inspiration, "why don't we go to Florida early this year—and stay a month."

"Is there money?"

"Of course," she said. "There's always money. Sometimes," she said wistfully, "I think I'd just like to be a beachcomber and live on the beach." She smiled. "Wouldn't that be lovely?"

Just then their son came tearing into the room. "Hey, Dad, you want to see my cowboy hat?"

"Hey, that's nifty. Come here though—the price tag's still on." Herman took it off, looked at it. "$49.50," he said. "Isn't that a bit expensive fcr a cowboy hat?"

"I read it wrong," she said. "I thought it was $4.95 till I got to the cash register. I didn't want to bother going back, standing in line again."

"She bought one for Charlie and Mike too."

"They came with us," she said. "I'd have hated to disappoint them."

That night Herman was unable to sleep. Bobbie had taken a sleep-ing pill and was lying inert beside him. But he was rest less, on edge. Whenever he was about to drop off, Eloise Moaks or H. T. broke in with their obscene gestures of love and death. Like sirens their voices wailed in his ears, blending with the sirens out-side that broke the night apart. He got up. He thought he'd try a sandwich—entice the juices of his brain down to his stomach, so to speak, to help him sleep. He stole out of bed and down the stairs. In the kitchen the canary-colored walls leaped out at him, while the orange-and-brown curtains framed panels of darkness. As he spread peanut butter on toast, the fluorescent lights that made the bronze stove and refrigerator glow eerily blue seemed to hold him under surveillance, as though he'd been caught in a forbidden act. Unnerved, he looked around suddenly, a stranger in his own house.

With the comfort of peanut butter, Herman walked into the living room to stand under the softer, more archaic light of Tiffany lamp shades. He felt a sense of pride when he walked into the liv-ing room, the dining room, the den, which reflected his work, and had brought his real talents into play: stripping paint from trim and wainscoting, restoring the fine old carved oak woodwork, reviv-ing the newel posts of the staircase. Then selecting the furnish-ings: the marble-top tables, the mahogany chest, the brocaded sofa, the great oak dining table. Some of his happiest moments had gone into making the house the showplace of the neighbor-hood, especially in laying out the garden.

When he and Bobbie were first married, poor and struggling,

they'd bought one of the older houses nobody wanted then. A beauty, a monument of the old aristocracy in the town. They'd put every cent into fixing it up. First they had done the downstairs, then the bedrooms. By that time they had more money; the children were old enough to choose their own decor, and the house seemed to take off beyond him. Gloria's room was a collage of posters of rock stars plastered over black walls, with strobe lights exploding with volleys of color while rock music blared and beat. Ricky's room was the inside of a spaceship, with panels of knobs on the walls for various games, and green Martians on the ceiling.

Just when everything had been finished, it was Bobbie's whim to turn one little unused space into a beauty room. They had spent hours at auctions so that they could recon struct the interior of a beauty salon of the Twenties, with hair dryers, mirrors, curling irons, and copies of old fashion magazines.

Astonishing what the house had become under his hands. It was as though a powerful agency had taken him over and moved through him. Nor was it finished. Now the third floor: bar, jukebox, fish tank. He had a sudden image of Bobbie swallowing the whole state of California and, moved by every wild and gathering impulse, being taken ever farther, to the point where one day she'd simply walk into the sky—a pink sky, flaring with rockets. But if that's what she wanted, then somehow he wanted it too. To make her happy—that's all he'd ever wanted to do. Just make her happy.

There were no sirens announcing the arrival of Dempsey Stringfellow and the firm's lawyer, George Meeker: merely a knock at the door of the blue house and the two of them emphatically, if quietly, on the front porch, in their three piece suits, carrying their briefcases.

"Forgive us for disturbing you," Stringfellow said, always the gentleman. "But Bobbie is home, I believe. We have some business to discuss with her."

"Of course," Herman said, a little surprised by the sudden materialization of those he knew only from the office Christmas party. He invited them to come in and wait. Bobbie was in the shower.

The men rose as she descended the stairs, as though to pay her homage—Meeker, a little groundhog of a man, who carried his shadow with him like a folded handkerchief; Stringfellow, lean and deeply tanned, with the kind of blond hair that takes in streaks of gray and seems never quite one or the other, and the good-looking boyface of a man used to being handsome and perfectly aware of his charm.

"Ah, Dempsey, George," she said. "What an unexpected surprise. But do sit down. Can I give you a drink?"

"How very kind," Dempsey said. "Perhaps another time."

"Then perhaps you won't mind if I have one," Bobbie said. "Herman?"

"No, no thank you," he said, a bit puzzled, for Bobbie never drank in the middle of the day. He looked into their faces for some clue as to their business. There was only some aimless chitchat until she had made her drink and come to rest in the Queen Anne chair by the fireplace.

Then, as though on signal, the lawyer began to speak. "During the last audit of our books," he began, "the accountant discovered a discrepancy, at first a careless error in the Laskey account. But then—he coughed delicately and cleared his throat—"on further investigation similar discrepancies appeared in some of the other accounts."

"What are you trying to say, George?" Bobbie demanded. "Dempsey, what is all this?"

Stringfellow, head back, tips of his fingers together, as if to dive or pray, unperturbed, said, "I think we're just stating a few facts. May we continue?"

Herman looked at his wife, who frowned and took a sip of her drink.

With a glance at his employer, a shift in his position, Meeker continued: "Owing to the frequency of the discrepancies," he said, "it appeared advisable to investigate further, to reexamine records of past years."

Although Bobbie had sat back in her chair in an attitude of ease, she seemed to give off little waves of heat. "What are you saying?" she flung at him.

"That you have embezzled well over a hundred and fifty thousand from the firm within the past six years," Stringfellow said. "Receipts not recorded, checks to phony accounts—it's all here," he said, patting the briefcase.

"It's a lie!" Herman protested. "It's a frame-up and a lie."

Ignoring him, Stringfellow turned to Bobbie. "You're a clever woman," he said, in a tone that did not begrudge her her talents. "You almost pulled it off." He allowed her to savor that possibility, then snatched it away. "But for one really glaring error, it might have gone on for years and years. The proof we have should stand up in any court, and though we could prosecute, we thought we might try something more . . . civilized." He appeared to be handing her a life-preserver. Would she accept or not?

"What are you suggesting?" she asked. "That I allow myself to be intimidated by all this nonsense?"

"I am suggesting," he went on patiently, "that the firm would gain nothing by letting you rot in prison—and there is something owing to the man who gave me my start." He did not appear to notice the glare this drew from Bobbie. "But if we can recover certain assets—" He was looking around: "House, furnishings, new car."

"Indeed," she said, standing up. "And do you think for one moment I'd submit to your blackmail? What unconscionable greed. It's not enough for you to swindle me at the beginning . . ."

Stringfellow and the lawyer had risen, as well as Herman, who was debating whether he should throw them out of the house.

"No doubt you'll want some time to think things over. I'd advise you not to leave town. Your choice is whether you want to go to court and face conviction or, as I said, some thing a bit more civilized. I thought for the sake of your family you might want to

154

avoid unpleasantness."

"How kind of you," she said, with deepest irony.

They left then. She watched them until they left the porch, then turned back into the room. For a moment she and Herman stared at each other across the space.

"Is it true?" Herman said, aghast.

"Do you believe them?" she said, with a smile. "Of course not."

"And if it were true," she said, "would you hate me?"

"What a question."

"If you didn't, then it would be only to get even with me. Torment me."

"What?" He was at a loss, trapped in a riddle. "Even if you did it, it wouldn't matter. We have each other." The formula sounded desperately trite.

"Well, it doesn't matter anyway," she said, "because they're not going to get away with it."

"Is it true?" he asked again. Somehow he had to know. She smiled as if her mind were elsewhere.

"But why then?" he said, assuming the worst. "We were doing all right."

"Is that all you can think of ?" She broke away from him, moved to the window. Savagely she plucked the dead leaves from one of the begonias. "When Daddy worked himself to the bone all those years and those jerks come along and make a killing . . ."

"They gave you your share."

"That's what you think. They knew the value of those as sets—way beyond what they told me. And I was so innocent God! Thinking they were all so broken up over Daddy, and how they were trying to do their best for his little girl. I was such a *fool*. Stringfellow knew. He had his finger on every thing. As soon as they paid me off, suddenly there were all those accounts I knew nothing about. Only *he* could get away with it." She was enraged.

"But you knew they'd find out sooner or later."

"Is that what makes them right, me wrong?"

He was stumped.

"And why should they have?" she said, reasonably. "There are millions of things people never find out—or don't find out till years later. And all the time they've been thinking they had the truth."

"Yes, but—"

"They don't even know yet how H. T. died," she threw in. "Maybe they never will. Suppose somebody killed him—had sat around planning it for years. There're lots of perfect crimes, lots of unsolved murders."

"But you'd know," he said, already tremulous with the discovery that that was the whole point.

"Of course," she said. "Suppose I did do it," she said, not granting him anything. "Why, I'd walk into that office every day thinking, I know something you don't know. I'd smile to myself every time I looked at them. I'd enjoy it. And all this," she said, "the results—I'd enjoy that too."

She meant it. That was clear to him. And she must have done it, though . . .

"But don't think they'll get away with it," she said. "They're just trying to pull a fast one."

He was completely bewildered.

"They just think they've found something out," she said.

The coroner was making a list of all those who had known H. T. Morgan and who had been with him at any time during the days just before his death. The question was who had seen him last. There was a brief flurry of excitement when one of the high school girls admitted to having visited him in his apartment the last day he was seen alive. They had drunk a beer together and passed a joint back and forth. There were brief rumors about whether or not she would be charged, but with what it was not exactly clear.

"Nothing," the coroner was saying to Herman. "Liver in excellent shape considering the way he was sloshing it down. No sign of heart attack or stroke. Wasn't electrocuted. For his age he was a healthy man." He shook his head. "There's nothing to go on. It has me stumped."

"Maybe he just died,"Herman said.

"People don't just die," the coroner said. "There's a cause. There's a reason."

Herman shook his head. He didn't know how to put it. "Maybe he couldn't live."

"That's no explanation," the coroner said, exasperatedly. "But what if you don't have a cause?"

"Then nobody'd ever die," he said, throwing up his hands. (They would though, Herman thought, for death was in the world. It didn't matter what you called it. For a moment he toyed with possibilities: ultimate combustion, spontaneous entropy, power failure, thanatotropism.)

"Don't you see," Cleaver went on, making one last effort to break through such thick-headed perversity, "that won't do at all. The public won't stand for it. They've got to have facts." He gave a sigh, perhaps of weariness. "Is there any other name you can give, anybody else who knew him?"

Herman shook his head. At least, with a perfect crime, you knew it was a crime. He knew nothing.

Maybe all you needed was a few facts on your side, Bobbie thought, but sometimes even that didn't do the trick. And when so much was at stake, you might as well play the game for all you're worth. She was excited, a little scared. A bit of a flutter in her stomach, a catch in her breathing. A quiet had settled over the house that magnified the slightest noise, sent a tremor through her. She strained her ears for some sound from the sleepers upstairs: Herman in the four-poster bed, Gloria among her rock stars, Ricky on his way to Mars. They would not wake; no, they mustn't wake. "I'll come to bed soon," she had assured Herman. "I'm too edgy right now. I couldn't possibly sleep. I'll relax with a drink."She would not let him stay up to keep her company; it would be better if she were alone. (Now when Herman came home in the evenings and stood before the blue house, it seemed scarcely real. He stood looking at it as though it might vanish in an instant, go up in a puff of smoke. Don't worry, Bobbie had said. They don't know what they're talking about. But something had happened. Nothing was the same. When he walked by H. T's little garage apartment, he saw a young couple moving in. It was as though H. T. had never lived there, had never been. And what had happened to all the years they had known each other . . . failed to know each other? The newspaper had reported finally that, according to the findings of the coroner, H. T. Morgan had been electrocuted by a faulty cord. So much for the public peace. Not that it made any difference.) Bobbie sat on the sofa in a peignoir, a magazine on her lap, turning pages: money-saving tips for meals, the latest fool proof diet, the most recent article on the Kennedys, ten ways to improve your sex life—it all passed before her eyes without interest or effect. Would she really be able to pull it off? Was it really going to happen? She had a sense of the possible, of the tremendous latent power that could make things go one way or another. If you could only get on top of it, make it go your way.

She heard a car approach and continue a little way down the block. She glanced at her watch: nearly one-thirty. She went to the window, drew the curtain back slightly, and peered out. Then she glided to the door, turned the knob ever so gently, and opened the door to let him in. He came inside, followed her as she motioned him into the little den off the living room. She closed the door behind them. That much at least was done.

"Well," Dempsey Stringfellow said, smiling at her with a certain benign satisfaction. "This is cozy. Can we talk?"

"Everybody's upstairs," she said. "Asleep."

"Good," he said. "I think there are things both of us want to say."

"You know what this has done to me," she said. "I'd do anything to keep from hurting Herman or the kids. It's all so overwhelming." The word came breathily, and she paused, for

158

the sake of magnitude, trying to get his mind to accept it. "The thought of losing the house, everything."

"Of course," he said, "I realize how much of a blow it is for you." His tone suggested that he was a man not without sympathy. Meanwhile, he was fingering a silver lighter on the antique carpenter's bench Herman had made into a coffee table.

"But that's not what I mean," she said, touching his arm. She waited for him to look at her. She had to have his full attention. She opened her hand. "What would I be without all of this?"

He moved toward her then and, drawing her close to him, ran his hand along the flimsy material of her peignoir, to her shoulder, above her breast. There he paused. "You'd still be—" He allowed his eyes, a curve of the lip, to do what mere words could not.

"What do you mean?" she demanded. "—desirable."

"Does that matter?" she said, lifting her eyes. It was not her only card, but since it seemed a good time to play it, why not?

"You know how I've always felt about you."

"Not exactly. And I'm not sure you understand."

"Of course I understand—how you've tried not to waste yourself—in this life, in this town. And I've admired you don't think I haven't. Your pizzazz. You've got it. And you've used it to take what you can get."

"But to hold onto it," she said with a smile. "That's the main thing." Then, so as not to sound too deadly serious, she said archly, ". . . if possible."

"And do you believe in possibility?" he asked, pressing her close to him, insinuating his hand between them.

"Of course," she said, raising her eyes. There was indeed something there she could make use of—not to be tossed off lightly. Maybe you could even dignify it by the notion of a philosophy.

"I love Herman," she said, drawing back, removing his hand, for it was distracting her. She had to keep a clear head. "Of course," he said, drawing her toward him again. "It would be terrible if you hated him."

"I don't want to hurt him," she said, looking up into his eyes, into the face that would never grow old. "And I don't want to be thrown into a corner like an empty beer can." She hoped it was a good line, not too rehearsed. She tried to gauge his reaction.

"Who does?" he said with a little smile.

"And do you know," she said, "I've always felt a kind of bond between us-that we wanted more than just . . . oh, you know what I mean."

"Yes," he said, smiling down at her, gently pushing aside a stray lock of hair on her forehead. "It's all a game, but you may as well have a little fun with it."

"So you can understand why, when you arranged for all the payments to come to you in cash, so that you could beat the IRS, I made my own copies of the receipts and noted carefully the names of the clients—just in case."

She thought she saw him blink at that. "Oh, you did that, did you?"

"Yes," she said. "And don't you think it might be bad for business if, say, the Nelson brothers and I. J. Green were accused of complicity?"

(Upstairs Herman was having a terrible dream: the house was filled with strangers, and all the furniture was on the lawn being auctioned off. Somebody had bought the four poster bed and the little bureau of burly walnut was going, going . . . He was looking everywhere in the crowd for Bobbie—walking up to people, asking where she had gone, but no one could tell him. He sat up, a cry ringing in his ears, but whether it was his own voice that had awakened him or a siren off in the distance he was unable to tell. He shook his head, trying to shake off the reality of the dream.)

"So it's all been a terrible mistake," she said with a smile. "And things will go on as usual, and nothing will mar the surface after all."

Though his face had gone red for a moment, he had recovered his composure. "You scheming little bitch," he said, almost allowing a chuckle of admiration to escape from his anger.

"And where did I learn it?" she said archly, putting her arms around him, holding him close, breathing in the scent of his Pour Lui. Now he could do as he liked.

REUNION

"Well, Jarve, you old sinner, it's about time," Alison said, as she met me on the porch. She gave me a little peck on the cheek, then stood back to make inspection. "You've gotten skinny as a rail, Jarve," she said, "and pretty thin on top. The years have begun to tell on you, Jarve."

"You haven't changed a bit, Al."

"Oh, yes, I know," she said, with a crack of a smile. "Same nasty tongue I've always had. But come in. No reason for us to stand on the porch staring at each other like idiots. Alna will be here directly to tell you how ill-used she always is." Before she turned to go in, she gave me another quick going over. "Little short of breath these days, are you?"

"I lost my cat."

"Oh?" she said, and pretended not to understand. "You derive long-windedness from cat fur? Cats make me sneeze." She sneezed. "Even the idea of cats."

"He was nearly wild in the car," I explained.

"I can imagine," she said, having noticed the covered bird cage next to my suitcase. "I can't say the bird would be too happy either. Must be continual warfare in the back seat worse than the battle of the sexes."

"A mynah bird," I told her. "He talks. Name's Charlie. But anyway—" going back to the cat, "the moment I opened the door, he shot out. Wouldn't come when I called. Stopped and gave me a backward look over the shoulder and hotfooted it off as fast as he could go. I tried chasing him ..."

"Just see he doesn't come in the house," she said. "I have put in my last cleaning up animal doo-doo." Then she added, "Foolishness to chase anything."

She ought to know, I thought: five-foot-four and over two hundred-fifty pounds. Already my malice was beginning to show. A bad sign. "Your personal philosophy?" I intended a dig.

"My personal philosophy," she said, underlining the words. "There is nothing in this world worth chasing—" She started in and held open the screendoor while I gave thought to whether I should hunt for Tigger or wait for him to turn up on his own. I followed her in.

"Nothing in this world—" she went on, "neither love nor fame nor ..."

"Truth?"

She snorted. "What's that anymore? No-'nor peace nor certitude nor light.' Spend your energy chasing around and all you get is a little pool of tears."

"Not getting cynical in your old age, are you, Al?" I said, upsetting a coat tree as I bumped it with a suitcase.

"Me? What an idea."

"That's an heirloom," she said, as I caught the coat tree on its way down to the floor. "Been in the family for at least three generations."

"Well, I'd hate to break up the family tree," I said, whatever that meant, and stood blinking in the hallway, unable to see a thing.

"We keep the blinds drawn for coolness," she said, raising one at the front-room window. Motes of dust danced in the sunlight. I settled myself in a wingback chair, while she lowered herself into an overstuffed.

"Well, you recognize the old place?" she wanted to know. "Think you can claim it?"

My eyes having adjusted to the light, the room began to take on a certain familiarity, though the furniture had been rearranged, a few things added, others gone. I crossed my legs, clasped my hands around my knee, and took a long look.

"That's Granddad's old school desk," she said. "They were going to get rid of it when they built the new school ... Used to be a huge big old double desk, but Alna and I had it cut in half so we could each have one."

Leather-covered couch, wooden rockers, overstuffed chairs,

163

the sort of things that would creak and scritch and groan when you sat in them, carrying on a conversation of their own, nearly all complaint. Dropleaf table with the milkglass plate and the shepherd and shepherdess exchanging coy looks across the polished surface. Family pictures on the wall, a crowd of silver and gold frames on the shelves, the desk, the mantel: including pictures of me. (But of course. The family never let go of you, never absolved you from being a member, but waited for the prodigal, who, in some sense, had never been allowed to leave.) Seth Thomas clock in the middle of the mantel, not running.

"Nothing's changed," I said. If anything new had been added, it had taken on the sentiment that stood behind the rest. The years she and Alna had kept the house, ever since Alna had become a widow, were a continuation of everything I could remember. The chairs had taken their shape; their feet had worn the design into the carpet, so that it was quite lost now. All the things there had been taken into the stream of their existence and become part of it. Nothing had really changed, but had just gone on, wearing down, wearing out. The room smelled of warmed sunlit dust. Suddenly sleepy, I had to fight down a yawn.

"It's smaller than I thought. I remember a much bigger house."

"It's big enough when you go to cleaning it. I've got so I don't want to clean up after anybody." She eased herself forward and heaved herself up out of the chair. "You can take a look around and freshen up while I get us a glass of something cold. I gave you your old room at the top of the landing."

Quite a bit smaller, I thought, and was almost afraid to look at my old room.

My room was under the eaves, corners cut out where the roof sloped down, the ceiling so low you always had the feeling you were going to bang your head. The house had settled badly, the door swinging wide of the frame, the floor like an inclined plane. I sat down on the white chenille spread, bedsprings squeaking, the mattress sagging into a hollow under me, and tried to see things clearly.

Some things happen under the sun; others are the gift of moonlight. And there are those that lie in the twilight that connects past and present—part dream, part memory. And here was the room I had lived in: brass bed, bookcase, desk, bureau. But now they stood out too clearly, like furniture in a secondhand store, with all their scars and scratches. Dream and memory fled before the eye of the large and obtuse stranger sitting in the boy's room. What connection had I to these objects that habit and sentiment, or the habit of sentiment, had preserved, not even really for me? Yet it was all there. Even a childish drawing tacked up on the wall. Where had they resurrected that from? I got up to look at it. It was a drawing of a man, but with wings where the arms ought to have been, as though I'd meant to draw an arm but the crayon had slipped and I'd drawn wings in order to make the best of a bad job. But the drawing intrigued me.

A good way to get past your mistakes, I thought. Fly beyond them. Fix on wings like you'd meant to fly. Make things look like you'd meant them to be that way and no other. Who'd know the difference? I'd know, I thought. I'd know. I'd been a damned fool and made a mess of things. Forget the wings if you don't know how to fly. I sat down on the bed again, staring down at the fragments of my life that lay around my feet. They stood in all the harsh glare that the room now did. Maybe some few things should be left unreclaimed in the twilight, seeing that you can't get rid of the others.

I thought of Winifred, the breakup of our marriage, and the bitterness that came of it. It's quite a shock to witness that sudden explosion of passion after so many years of numbed feeling, like finding sudden life in a deadened nerve. You can be full of cynical blame—I was for a time. But what minute un spoken adjustments we must have made for each other over the years. My silence behind a newspaper or book; her absorption with the coffee hour after church, the sewing group, the bridge games. For each other we had the bills, the weather, the local gossip.

You come to the end of such things and finally you call them by their true name—failure. If s like living with fading eye sight or a loss of hearing. It happens so gradually you don't notice, till one day the world is in shadow and no birds sing. Then you know only what is lost, not how to get it back. You look at the woman who has put the peanut butter or the cheese spread on all those slices of bread, and opened up her legs at night—and you know failure.

I had reached the point where I couldn't blame Winifred, though she took everything—the house, the furniture, the good car, the savings. I hadn't wanted any of it. Now that the life had flowed out of it, it was a bunch of rubbish, the flotsam of thirty years. The old wreck of a car, a few hundred dollars, the cat, and the bird were all I had left.

I avoided all my friends and acquaintances; didn't want to talk to anybody. I shed my old life like a wrinkled skin. I took the cat and the bird and moved into the Petite Apartments, one of the great old homes brutally subdivided in a neighbor hood on the downslide from respectability. You made your way up to the porch past the garbage cans and the tricycles and toys lying in the middle of the sidewalk and all over the porch and entered into a decaying hallway. Just in time for a wife or kid getting slapped around or a hair-pulling fight among a couple of the women: shrieks and curses, cries and blows. After a while it became just so much background noise, just as the smells of everybody's supper were simply the air you breathed. And even the faces . . . Who noticed? Except when the cops came looking for somebody who'd forged checks or skipped out on his bills. By that time, long gone. Faces changed, but nothing else. For a time, a little girl named Rachel knocked on my door every morning wanting milk, some thing to eat—her mother was always sick or asleep. Then they too were gone and I was left to myself.

I had the idea that Tigger, Charlie, and I were going to create a new life together. I tried to get the cat and bird to become friends and companions. I'd hold Tigger on my lap and pet him till he purred. Then I'd reach over and bring Charlie out of his cage, a little closer each time. I could tell Charlie was pretty nervous about the whole idea. But Tigger would just lie there and purr, with only a little twitch in the stick end of his tail.

One day I went out and left the two of them together, Charlie in his cage, which was hanging from the ceiling, and Tigger curled up in the chair. When I came back, Tigger was up there with Charlie, in mid air with no place to go, hanging onto the cage with all his claws. He'd leapt up from the table. I'd have been impressed by the leap if I hadn't been so quick to judge him. I gave him a cuff or two as I dropped him to the floor. He laid back his ears and whipped under the bed. After that he kept clear of me. Came in for his food, but that was it. The hunting was too deep in his blood for him to give it up, even for the sake of society. It was my fault. I'd been living in a dream. Trying to create the Peaceable Kingdom. But the cat wasn't ready to lie down with the mynah bird, and I'd have done better to get down on all fours myself.

About that time two things happened: an old woman, the only permanent renter of the Petite Apartments, died, and I figured out the nature of the smell in the hallway. The old woman was ninety-one, and she hated so much to spend a penny that she'd starved to death. Under her bed they found a can with $35,744.32 inside. The smell in the hallway I'd got ten so used to was of many things rolled up in one: sweat and dirt and the damp behind the plaster, diapers soured in the pail and boiled cabbage and potatoes fried in lard. I hadn't been able to figure out what the smell was. But after the old woman died, suddenly I knew: it was the smell of failure and slow death. And when I knew that, I fled—back up here. Home.

"Jarve, come down and have some lemonade." Alison. Then another voice. "Jarvis, guess who's here."

It was Alna. I left the suitcase half unpacked and went downstairs.

"Oh, Jarvis, Jarvis," Alna said, devouring me in her arms, smothering me in her bosom, giving me a great wet sisterly kiss. "You've come back to us. You're a sight for sore eyes. Though I know you can't say the same of me. The years have been too hard on me,

167

Jarve . . ."

I tried to protest. Actually the years had left her a great soft rubbery mound, like her twin. Little red eyes that seemed on the verge of weeping, peering timidly from a great billow of fat. She seemed ageless; the skin of her face was as smooth as an infant's.

"Don't say anything good about her," Alison put in, handing me a glass of lemonade. "She'll only have to work harder denying it."

"How long has it been, Jarve, since you've come to a reunion?" Alna said, as we sat down. "How wonderful you've come now—just in time. I used to think, He doesn't like us any more, doesn't want to have anything to do with us . . . "

"Now, Alna," I said, thinking, Here we go again. "People drift apart. They get busy and . . . "

" . . . stop caring any more," Alison said, perfunctorily—reminding me of all the reasons I had stayed away.

"But now we have him back," Alna said—she'd had to draw a little blood. With a little guilt I could pay the price of reentry into her affection. "For the first time since before Corey's wedding. And you've never seen the babies—Annie and John and David or any of Dodie's kids, and . . . "

"I suppose Aggie will come," Alison said.

"Of course she will," Alna said, almost belligerently. "Why shouldn't she come?"

"Aggie has a new husband," Alison explained. "Smaller than the last. The only kind she marries are the ones she can pick up and throw."

"Well, it could have been worse," Alna said. "Just thank your lucky stars . . ."

"And worse it may be yet. The worst is not so long as we can say 'This is the worst.'" With a little smile she challenged us to match her book-learning.

"I see you can still bring out the Bard with the best of them," I said. "Well, I've been away a long time. I've lost track of my connections." All of them. Even Alna's three girls—Corey, Dodie, and Aggie. Girls? Women now, still stuck with the same ridiculous nicknames they'd been saddled with as children. The youngest, Corey, had been like my own daughter. She was in fact the same age as my older girl, and when she was little she used to come down and stay with us now and then. Corey liked what she called "adventures," and traveling a hundred miles or so on the bus by herself was an adventure. That had been a long time ago. It was hard to bring everything up to date. Marriages, kids, divorces, second marriages, what-all.

"Well, you went away," Alison said, as though pointing out a moral fault. "The rest of us stayed behind mostly. They go," she said, perhaps to someone not present, but listening, "though I don't know that they're any better off for it. You look like you've been picked clean down to the tail feathers, Jarve," she said, with her usual bite. "You look like you came here on the run."

"You're a balm to the spirit, Al." Yes, indeed. Coming back had its price. And how long did one go on paying?

"All I do is speak out what everybody else is afraid to say."

"Some people think they're being honest," Alna said, "when all they're being is disagreeable."

Alison looked at her in surprise. "That's pretty good," she said. "You're not going to get clever on us in your old age—"

"But the important thing," Alna said, sheering off, "is that he's here—with us. And he'll stay, and it'll be just like it was before she took him away from us—using her Daddy's hardware store as a bait and a lure. Grandma never got over it."

"And what does that say about me?" I demanded.

"I'll bet she took you for plenty," Alison said.

"Come now," I said, "you've looked for reasons to dislike Winifred ever since I first brought her home. Whatever she took, I let her take."

"The more's the pity."

"She was never our sort," Alna said. "I knew things would work out like this."

"But Alna," I protested, trying to keep my temper, "it was

169

thirty years. We had a whole life together."

"Pooh," she said, waving her hand, the fat of her upper arm quivering. "A woman knows those things. And I knew how anxious she was to marry our little brother. She didn't have the connections. And when the girls came along and she saw they'd be eligible . . . "

"Eligible?"

"For the DAR. For the FFV."

"What are you talking about?" I said, raising my voice. "Where did you get such an idiotic notion?" It was awful—I hadn't been home an hour and already I was shouting.

"What have I done?" Alna wailed.

'I'm sorry. Please—just forget I said anything."

"You can hardly blame him," Alison said, turning on her as well. "Who cares about such rubbish? It's all down the drain anyway."

And with a sweep of her hand, she dismissed my past like a pan full of dirty water.

The next day was Memorial Day, the day the family reunion was always held, and half the county was on hand for the event. For everybody in those parts was connected to everybody else, and you were always discovering some new member of the family who'd staked a claim on the remote borders of kinship. Seemed like hardly anybody ever left the area, but instead married and settled down to add another set of cousins to the total. And those few who picked up stakes to go back East or out West might as well have been numbered among the wayward, the lost, or the dead. All during the morning people kept swarming in and out of the house, the little kids chasing one another around a yard brilliant with roses and daylilies, while the teenagers stood off to one side, deep in themselves. Meanwhile their folks drank coffee and visited, carrying on as though they hadn't seen one another for years, though half of them lived less than twenty miles away.

In years past, the picnic had been held in the park right on the bank of the Tippicanoe River, which makes a wide lazy bend right through the center. But, now that Corey had her new house and lots of space, they held the picnic there. I hadn't seen Corey yet; I was anxious to know how she'd turned out, she'd been such a favorite of mine.

"We'll go over early," Alna said, "so you can have a chance to see the cemetery. Harley's done a lot with it."

"That so?" As far as I knew, there was only one thing you could do with a cemetery.

I'd been wondering what sort of man Corey had ended up with. I hadn't gone to her wedding. Guess I was afraid to. Corey had wanted to go off to college in California, but Alna wouldn't let her: she could go to college right here at home if she wanted to go. But Corey always had had a stubborn streak—said that if she couldn't go where she wanted, she wouldn't go at all. Next thing I heard she was getting married. About noon Harley himself came over to fetch Alna. I was to take Alison in my car. This was so that each could sit in the front seat, since it would have baffled the ingenuity of any driver to get either of them in or out of the back seat. Neither could drive, and Harley's was a two-door model.

Harley was a short burly fellow with carrot-colored hair and a round amiable face, rather mealy and freckled the way of so many redheads. He shook hands with a grip that fell just short of mashing together all the bones in my hand and gave me a smile from a toothpaste ad.

"Been up since six," he announced. "Had to open a grave and wanted to get it done before folks started coming and bringing their flowers. Wouldn't have looked right." He was proud of the fact that he was about the only one around who opened graves "by hand" any more. And he showed me his arm, which was as thick and solid as the average man's leg. "Feel that," he said. "Hard as a rock. It's what comes of digging graves. I can dig one in an hour. If you tried it, or most folks, you'd be in one."

"Harley, you're bragging," Alison said. He grinned and rocked back on his heels.

"Don't know what we'd do without Harley," Alna said. "He does all the yard work, and whatever breaks down he puts back together. He can fix anything."

"By the way, Harley," Alison said, "we're having trouble with the sink letting out. Gone sluggish again. It's probably tree roots in the sewer."

"I'll check it over right now. I've got my tools in the car—always keep 'em handy." And he dashed off to get them. "Obliging fellow, I will say that for him," Alison said.

Alna took this as a cue for praise: Harley was not a man to sit idle. He was strong as an ox and cheerful as a sunbeam. He built houses and dug graves and carved monuments and worked part-time for an electrician. Never idle.

"Not one of your types to sit behind a desk exercising a pencil," Alison said, in time for Alna to add: "You can say that again."

"Yes," Alison said, "Harley is a man who knows what he wants and knows how to get it."

Which was more than I did.

And he stood there entirely at home with himself, Alna beaming over him, her son-in-law, and Alison willing to make use of him.

"I'll ream her out this afternoon while you all are playing canasta."

"You've got a lot of energy," I said—which was true. "Everything he touches turns to money," Alna said, admiringly.

"He's got the first nickel he ever made," Alison said to me as we were going out. "He'll be a rich man any minute now." As we drove down Grant Street with its great old houses, Alison reminded me of the families that had lived in them nearly half a century ago. She remembered all the names of those who, for me, had slipped out of sight and memory, the kids we'd played with and gone to school with, and what had happened to them since and who they'd married and where they'd gone. Since I'd left, the town had spread out in all di rections, frantically adding new developments as though it couldn't wait to become a city. I hardly recognized the old center of town.

The families were gone from the old houses, where signs indicated the nests of lawyers, doctors, real-estate brokers, and insurance agents that had taken over, installed paneling and wall-to-wall carpeting, and set up for business.

We left the houses behind and traveled along a dirt road for perhaps half a mile.

"You remember the old part of the cemetery," Alison said, "where all the Butterworths and Waggoners are buried Great-uncle Jed and Frank as well as Granddad. Mom and Dad are at this end just on the other side of the road."

"Which part is Harley's?"

"That's on past. Can't see it for the hill. He bought the land to make a private cemetery. Only the town was running out of room and wanted to buy it from him. He was too smart to sell. So now the town leases the land from him, and he's grave digger, caretaker, the whole works. Here, turn up this drive." We drove up to a large ranch-style home, set right on the top of the hill, commanding a view of the green swath below, where artificial wreaths made gaudy spots of color on the grass. Corey's house. Harley had built it himself. Not only did it have all the modem conveniences, but, as Alison said with her usual irony, it had the advantage of being close to his work. I helped Alison from the car, and we walked to the door accompanied by the chimes of "Rock of Ages," being piped out by an amplifier on the corner of the house.

"Oh, Uncle Jarve," Corey cried when she saw me, throwing her arms around my neck. "Oh, it's so wonderful to see you. Come in."

She gave Alison a quick kiss. "I tell you those kids are about to wear me out. This is John," she said, giving the little boy a twitch on the shoulder. He was about five—carrot-colored hair like his dad's. "Now you take your truck outside and be have yourself and tell David to behave. Where's Mother any way?" she demanded of Alison. "Why isn't she around when you need her? Make yourselves at home," she said in a hurried way. "I've got to see about the potato salad. Go on now," she said to John, "and you stay right where I can keep my eye on you."

"She's on tranquilizers," Alison said in a low voice, "though what earthly good they're doing I can't imagine. Come," she said. "We can take a little walk before things get started. Bundle of nerves," she murmured.

When we got outside, Harley and Alna had come up. "You'd better go in and lend some aid and comfort to your daughter," Alison said.

I let Alison lead me off, so that I wouldn't allow myself to dwell on the disappointment I felt deep within. Corey, this harried woman? Was there anything left of the Corey I remembered?

Alison knew the cemetery the way she knew the town. A living archives. And she ticked off the graves one after another. "That's Greatuncle Jed buried there. He lived to be the oldest—105. The Ridpaths are nearly all of them over here. Three of Granddad's brothers. The other one went West and was never heard from again."

"So there was one of them who left," I said.

"There's always a restless one or two in every lot. And there's Granddad."

"Josiah Ridpath," I read. A good strong name, I thought, trying to make out the dates where the weather had discolored the stone. Name for a patriarch, builder of a line. For his time he'd been an outstanding person. Educated man, farmer, superintendent of schools when the Democrats were in power; teacher, when they weren't. The family still voted Democrat it was a tradition. And he'd sent both my father and his brother to college. "Maybe they knew what they were doing when he was alive."

"You think so?" Alison said. "When have people ever known what they were doing? And I remember what he was like. You were too young. He took up all the room, and the rest of the world was background and decoration. Oh, he was civic-minded all right. But when did Grandma ever have a thought of her own?"

"He lived by his lights," I said. "You have to say that for him."

"Yes, a man of principle. Stubborn and high-minded. When in doubt, do right. Well, I suppose you save a lot of confusion and wasted energy."

A rock—that's what he was. To be relied on. Even his memory had something hard and substantial about it, monumental. Maybe that's why I came back. What would he have thought looking at me? ("Degenerate sons and daughters, life is too strong for you.") The same thing he must have thought about my dad, very likely. Who had gone off to college bearing the hopes of the family, but who, instead of becoming the minister they reckoned on, threw away his life to become a musician. Even went off to New York for a time. But he came back finally, unable to earn a living, and became organist for the local Methodist church, giving lessons on the side and playing the violin for occasional evening gatherings. Died not long after I was born. And now here I was. Aloud I said, "Once I had the right way. Now I don't seem to have any way. Guess you're the clear-sighted one in this generation. You haven't botched things up the way some of us have."

"No, I s'pose not. I just get to watch the rest of the world go at it—that is my exalted privilege."

By the time we got back to the house, little clusters of people were all over the yard, with fresh arrivals coming up the hill every minute. The picnic tables had been set up alongside the garage, paper plates and napkins weighted down with pickle jars and catsup bottles to keep the breeze from sweeping them down the hill. The tables were loaded with food: chicken and noodle casseroles with crust on the top and gravy oozing through, and piles of ham and fried chicken and pots of baked beans and marshmallow jello salads and macaroni salads and coleslaw and creme pies and cherry pies and angel food cakes and pans of brownies and a great lovely strawberry shortcake with whipped cream on the top. A real winner. I had staked that one out right away, wondering how I could grab a piece before everybody else beat me to it. And right as I had my eye on it, Corey's boy John reached up and took a fistful out of the top, as much cake and strawberry as he could grab.

"John! You little beast! What have you done?"

John, struck with mortal terror by the voice that had come suddenly out of nowhere, stood glued to the spot, did not even put his fistful of strawberries into his mouth. He just stood there while Corey dashed out of the kitchen and whacked him hard on the side of the head. He stumbled as she yanked him into the house bawling, a smear of whipped cream across his cheek

Some few looked up from the conversations, then went back to talking. None of their affair. But something contracted inside me, and suddenly all the fried chicken and ham and salad and beans and pies and cake that you could dive into and come out on the other side of , feeling cheerful and at one with all those folks tied to you by the bond of kinship, was just food. Still I heaped up a plate with everything it would hold and ate it all down like food was going out of fashion; and then it all sat there like lead on my stomach, pulling me to the downhill side of the afternoon.

I was weary. I'd just about worn out my jaw. No sooner did I lift the fork to my mouth than somebody would ask me a question and I'd have to fill him in about my history. And there, fresh in memory, were all the things I would have been glad to forget. But that wasn't the worst. I had to listen to all the codgers who knew everything that had ever happened in the family and who could not forget or leave out a single scrap. "Your daddy was tall and skinny like you. Sickly. And when you were growing up . . . " History was everywhere. I was in the middle of it, no escaping. All down the hill it lay. And I felt giddy, like I was being absorbed backward into it, devoured by ghosts.

I sought comfort in the present generation. I found my other niece, Dodie, with her kids in tow, who looked a comfortable matron, rather heavy, working on a double chin. I learned the names of the kids and the grades they were in, I heard about their new house and her husband's job, and then we took refuge in the weather. There was nothing more to talk about.

"Where's Aggie?" I asked. "I haven't seen her yet." Dodie

shrugged. "Ah, you can never tell about Aggie. She may turn up or she may not"—as though it were all the same whatever she did.

"And I don't see Corey. I'll bet she hasn't even eaten yet." That gave me a chance to escape. If I went inside the house, at least I wouldn't have to talk to anybody for a while. Or else I could talk to Corey, if that's where she was. I hadn't seen her since she dragged the little fellow off. I found her sitting on the lounge in the living room with the child beside her. He was asleep. His face was flushed from crying and every now and then his breath would catch in a sob and send a tremor through his sleep. I could see that Corey had been weeping.

"What's the matter, honey?"

"I don't know why I hit him like that," she said, the tears streaming down her cheeks. "I must be crazy." She dabbed at her eyes with the wadded remains of a Kleenex. "What did it matter if he took a hunk out of the cake? Seems like every time they do anything all I know to do is beat on them."

I sat down beside her and took her hand. "It's hard raising kids. You never know whether to blame yourself for the things you've done or the things you didn't do." Then I thought: That's a helluva lot of comfort.

"Oh, why am I so terrible?" she said. "I feel so restless. I fly off the handle at nothing—I feel like I want to hit somebody or break something."

I held her hand without saying anything. What was I supposed to tell her? To get some hobbies or improve her bridge game? What had happened to her? She'd been such a great kid—wonderful. Where had it all leaked away? And why? I had to ask it, even though I was hardly in any position to think: She's a disappointment to me.

"Something's wrong with me," she said. "It just seems like I'm missing—oh, I don't even know what. Oh, Uncle Jarve, it's terrible not knowing—driving me crazy. Maybe if I'd gone away and been to college like I wanted, I'd know. Oh," she cried, leaning on my shoulder. "I'm an old woman, and I'm not even thirty."

She dabbed at her eyes again and blew her nose. "I'm glad

you're here," she said. "You're the only person . . ." Then she turned to me with an expression I recognized from her child hood: serious, full of question, as though she'd been turning something over in her mind for a long time and now had to have a straight answer. "You went to college, you went away . . . " she began.

"But all I ever did was run a hardware store," I said, "in another little town. As for my education—it kept me away from the *Reader's Digest Condensed Books* and allowed me to concoct my own set of private miseries as a reaction to what's wrong with the world."

"But why did you come back?"

"I don't know, honey," I said, genuinely puzzled. "I guess I was scared, maybe scared enough to forget the reasons I'd left in the first place."

"Are you going to stay, Jarve?" she said, looking at me intently. When she said it, dropping the "uncle" and looking at me like that, it was as though some part of myself was sitting in front of me putting me to the test.

"I don't know, honey."

I had to get up at that point and move around. Why had I left? Why had I come back? What was I going to do? "I guess there's always been something in me that could never get along in the world," I said, thinking out loud. "Especially when I was a kid. There was always something else, at the back of my eyes that I could see, even if it wasn't really there—like a dream. I thought it was gone. But I think it's always been there, even under all the patchwork and fabrication I've been putting on top of it for the past quarter of a century—God, it's been longer than that."

"A dream," she said excitedly, "and you still have it?"

"I guess." If that's what you could call the dissatisfaction, the restlessness, the itch in the blood. If you could glorify it with the name *dream*. I thought I'd outgrown it, whatever it was; thought the surface of my life had got too much of a deposit on it for anything to break through. But now that all was cracked and broken and the darkness had welled up, was there reason to hope for light?

"Then you won't stay," she said. "Oh, I knew it."

"Hold on, wait a minute." She was about to snatch the rug out from under me. "Where can I go, for God's sake?"

"Oh, thank you, Jarve."

"Thank you for what?" There was a taste of acid in my mouth.

"You give me hope. You make me believe I don't have to be a failure."

I could have wept. "All you're thanking me for is misery for troubles you can't even give a name to."

"Oh, you make me want to hug you." No doubt she would have if the child hadn't been on her lap.

From outside, somebody said, "Where's Corey? Haven't seen her all afternoon."

"They'll come in," she said, gathering up the child, who had sat up and was rubbing his eyes. "Come on in to the bathroom, honey. Tell them I'll be out in a bit," she said, and carried him quietly down the hall.

"Where's Corey?" Alna said, coming in, Harley right on her heels. "She's missing all the fun. Soon as everybody clears out, we'll have a little canasta."

"I'm going on over to see about the sewer," Harley said, "soon as I get out of these clothes."

"You'll miss all the fun," I said.

"My work's my pleasure," he said with satisfaction, and left me only the comfort of a nice bit of irony.

"You'll have to explain things to me," I said. "I haven't played this game for years." And didn't want to now. With a little less sleep and a rawer state of nerves, I might have made it as far as hatred and violence. As it was, I settled for a sort of low grade irritability. Corey and I both had been roped into playing. We made suitable partners.

"Pooh, it's simple," Alison said. "Even we can play it." "Al's used to winning," Corey said.

"Well now, don't discourage him at the outset," Alison said. "I haven't got luck trapped in a corner."

'I've never seen anybody like her," Corey said. "The cards go her way."

The discard pile was beginning to mount as we kept going round the table. And the tension was building. Even I got into the game. The cards kept mounting up—nobody had enough to meld-to the point where the pile was worth taking. So I took it. Alison discarded a five; I had two of them and the points to open.

"Now look at that," Alna said.

"Yes, just look at that," Alison said. "I had my eye on that stack. Been sitting here with the points just waiting for the right card." And she reached over and pinched me.

A right sharp pinch, as though she'd meant it to hurt, and she sat there looking ruffled and displeased. Why, she really does want to win, I thought, spreading out another run. And my blood was up—I wanted to beat her just for the sake of triumph. Now there was real zest in the play that seemed to raise both sight and hearing almost to animal keenness. I became aware of Alison's breathing, even thought I could hear her heart pumping. And there was Corey taking the next fat pile, which included Alna's joker, a sacrifice.

"Now look at that, will you," Alison said, giving me another pinch. "Why, they mean to take everything."

"Not leaving anything for us," Alna moaned.

And I thought: If I take that pile again, the buttons will pop off the front of her dress. It was worth working for. Ah, joy of battle!

"I got it this time," Alna said, swooping up the pile gleefully.

But it was thin pickings.

"At least we'll have a book of tens. They won't romp all over us."

"And I'm going to make two more black canastas," Alison said, "before they go out."

When the hand ended, we were far ahead, and the next two went with a rush of luck for Corey and me. I glanced over to see what the score was, but we were ahead by a surprisingly small mar-gin—only about fifteen hundred points. Had she added wrong? No, Alison never added wrong. We were winning, but now I had to beat them mercilessly. We had to take the pile every chance we got.

"Oh, Uncle Jarve," Corey said. "You're doing wonderfully.

I bet we're over three thousand points ahead." That didn't help matters.

"You just wait," Alison said. "You just wait." She was drumming her fingers on the table, so I thought I was reasonably safe. Then I nearly leapt from the table, she pinched me so hard. Alna got me from the other side.

The pile was building up again, and Alna and Alison, sitting across from each other, were two great cats watching it with narrow eyes, waiting . . .

"Hello, everybody, here I am. Where's all the food?" Opening the door, sweeping into the room like a hot wind, there was Aggie. She was carrying a sackful of lettuce, which she set down on the floor. "Well, Uncle Jarve. Fancy meeting you here. They've roped you into a card game already." She plopped herself into a chair and sat rocking back and forth. Heavy-breasted, her knees spread apart, she gave the impression that she was enjoying herself hugely.

"Why, Aggie," Alna said, "what are you doing here this time of day?"

I had seen Alna flinch when she came in, a protest of flesh, an unconscious squirm with a long history. For Aggie had been a wild child and not a credit to the family. It was rather a miracle she'd graduated from high school, before flunking out or being kicked out. Whooping it up half the night on the back roads with the boys, coming to school the next day and sleeping on her desk. Flinging into class in a skimpy blouse, barefooted, bells around her ankles, and being sent home with stern warnings. Yelling across the study hall to her drama teacher, her favorite, "Oh, Ella, Aunt Ella, I'm pregnant. What'll I do?" Running off with a folk-singer right after graduation; returning home three years later with a child and no husband. A second marriage, a third, a fourth.

And still untamed. All that lay behind Alna's squirm.

"You're only half a day late," Alison said. "Didn't think you'd be coming."

"Neither did we. Elton'll be here in a minute. I brought eggs——hen eggs and goose eggs. You should see my gray geese. Proud and fat. Strut all over the yard." She got up, put her arms akimbo and strutted around the room. "My gray geese are like my children."

"And your children?" Alison said, dryly. "What are they like?"

"Well, Auntie," she said, not the least abashed. "I haven't even seen them for three years now. The abandoned little orphans. They're well taken care of. Henry can feed 'em and clothe 'em same as I."

"I wish I could take things as lightly as you. Run off devil-may-care."

"It's a gift, Auntie," she said, and laughed. "Now I have my gray geese and my teddy bear. Come in, love."

Her teddy bear was a thin little runt of a man, whose hair shot off into a cowlick at the back of his head. He held out a limp damp paw for me to shake and pumped my hand a time or two, gave a little nod and a friendly grunt, and sat back on the couch, having done his bit for sociability. Aggie dwarfed him, both in size and voice; she boomed-she filled a room. Whatever her other husbands had been, this time she had pawed around in the back patches of Mother Nature till she'd found one witless and pliable enough to do her bidding.

"Now bring in the eggs, Elton," she said, "and mind you don't drop 'em."

"How are things with you, Aggie?" Corey asked.

"Can't complain. Put in tobacco again this year. The allotment's small, but it'll be worth money. Got a little corn and a little alfalfa. Got a pig and three goats and half a dozen sheep and a cow and the gray geese. I work from first light till nearly dark. See my hands," she said, holding them out. "Rough from digging in the dirt."

"Honest work," Alison said, though which way her irony cut was hard to tell.

"Yes, Auntie. I was always the one for clean living." She broke into a great peal of laughter.

Elton came in with the eggs and took them into the kitchen.

We'd stopped playing when Aggie came in, but there was no move to break up the gaine. "Discard," Alna said. "You're holding up the gaine," Alison said. So I played.

"There's food in the kitchen," Corey said. "Plenty left in the refrigerator. Just help yourselves."

They both brought in plates of food and ate it and talked while we continued to play cards. Then, quite as abruptly as she had come in, Aggie stood up to leave. "Well, we got to be going," she announced. "Going to have us a little night out. No, don't anybody get up, we can find our way to the door." Actually nobody had made a move in that direction. "Come, love. 'Bye all. Just wanted to pay our respects to the family. Have fun, Uncle." She gave me a wink and swept out of the room, Elton in tow, carried along, it seemed, by the power of her voice alone.

"Well, she seems to be getting along all right with her new husband," Alna said, determined to stay on the sunny side of life.

"I should hope so," Alison said. "Why she'd squash him flat if he looked at her the wrong way."

Alna's face flushed.

"Aggie never had any moral sense," Alison went on, freezing the pile.

"She never had any sense, period," Corey said.

"I raised my girls to be good girls," Alna protested, close to tears.

"Well, Aggie ducked out on you—ducked out on the teacher and the preacher both."

All that energy, I thought. Given the right direction she ought to have been able to fly to the moon.

"She's a disgrace," Corey said.

"That may be," Alison said. "But she's also your sister."

"Yes, I have to remember that, don't I? Because you'll put me

183

down if I forget."

"Don't be impertinent, miss," Alison said, as though Corey were nine years old.

"She *is* a disgrace," Corey insisted. "Not to the family or to me—you think I care about that? She's a disgrace to herself."

It was as though all her frustration and pent-up feeling had been suddenly magnetized by Aggie's appearance. Now it filled the room, and Alna and Alison were staring at her as though she'd gone crazy: she was making a spectacle of herself .

"And what might you know about that?" Alison said, tact less-ly.

"And what right do you have—?" Corey yelled, roused to fury. "You can't even add."

"What?"

"You added the score all wrong. We have another 700 points you didn't give us, plus all the rest."

"Corey!"Alna said, "How dare you?"

"It's true. I've always known. And I've been watching." Turning to Alison. "I know how you win."

Though she made an effort to seem composed, Alison was visibly shaken. "Coretta Jean, I'm going to leave this house and I'll not come back until—"

"Until what?" Corey said, pushing back the chair, standing up. "Until I get down on my knees and beg?"

"Well, I got the roots out," Harley announced triumphantly, man against nature. He'd come in so quietly through the back door we hadn't heard him. There he was, smiling, grease and dirt on his clothes and hands, a smudge of grease across his forehead.

Corey looked at him, made a gesture as though it was all hopeless.

"Well, I guess I don't look like an icecream salesman," he said.

"Oh, go clean up," Corey said.

"What's the matter, honey?" he said, bewildered. "What'd

you expect a man to look like who's been cleaning out a sewer."

"Will you clean up, you big slob," she said, sweeping the cards off the table. "Mother, I'll drive you home. I want to talk to you."

Harley's face paled, leaving his freckles without any visible means of support.

Alna was weeping. "How could you do that? How could you?"

"Goddam it to hell," Corey yelled.

"What's wrong?" Harley wanted to know. "What's happened?"

"O God," Corey whispered. "O God."

The house originally owned by my grandparents and now inhabited by the twins had never been what you would call fancy. Not one of those fine old houses with gingerbread along the porch and stained-glass windows along the stairwell or leaded glass in the front door. New, it had been ordinary; now it was old, with a patchwork of things done to it to keep it standing—asbestos shingles laid over the weathered exterior, aluminum storm-windows installed with the hope of reducing the drafts, a new electric stove put in the kitchen, but the same old plumbing endlessly repaired. From time to time a new layer of wallpaper over the old, a new coat of paint on the woodwork. Ordinary, comfortable, threadbare, but hanging on. Only now when we got back, there was an air of desolation about it, what with each person cut off from the rest by feelings too powerful for himself, let alone anybody else.

Alison and I got back long before Corey brought Alna home. I lay down for a while, heavy and depressed, and dozed off. When I woke it was fully dark outside. I sat up, shook my head free of sleep, then got up without turning on the light. For a time I stood looking out the window, trying to put something together. Family. Granddad. The twins. I couldn't put any thing straight, couldn't line them up like portraits along a wall. Corey's outburst reverberated in my head. Loss. Waste. Betrayal. My father. And I. Who, what were the failures? And which was worse—the betrayal of others or of oneself?

I became aware of a confused babble of voices rising from below, wail and argument: Corey and Alna. "I want to be something," I heard from one of the outbursts, "before I'm buried."

In the quiet that followed, I heard Alison say, "A celebrity? A femme fatale?"

I heard the door slam, and the house settled into silence. I turned on the light and sat down on the edge of the bed. I don't know how long I sat there not thinking of anything, until realized that I had been staring at the winged man. It was a curious creature with its triangular wings and a face too innocent even for hope. Had the boy merely been attempting to leap past a wrong move? Or had he been yearning toward some as yet unguessed possibility? And had the man unknowingly brushed past it, let it slip away all unheeded? Forever gone. Or might one still …? I hardly dared ask the question and yet not to ask it … O God, I thought. The waste. The terrible waste.

I continued to sit there over an inward groan. And what was the good of sitting there? I wanted to know. If I was going to botch things up, hell, I might as well do a job of it. Perhaps Corey at least . . . And if she believed in what I could scarcely believe in myself . . .

I went to the closet and pulled out my suitcase. Now was as good a time as any. When I went downstairs, Alna and Alison were in the living room, sitting opposite one another in the overstuffed chairs. Alna was crying.

"All my children have treated me this way—like dirt. And their father, out of his mind half the time."

"Well, you married him," Alison reminded her, "against the wishes of the family. And went on living with him—"

"Oh, how can you—when I'm in all of this trouble? Her just leaving him flat out. A good marriage, the children, that beautiful home."

"Well," Alison said, "they're all doing it these days. Life goes on, eh, Jarve.?"

"Well, you're the philosophical one," I said, on my way to the door. Alison looked at the suitcase but didn't comment.

"With a house like that, you'd think she could put up with anything," Alna wailed.

"Maybe she should have gone to California like she wanted," Alison said, her voice following me out the door, "and got all the nonsense worked out of her system."

"You're the one who always knows the right thing to do," Alna cried, "—for everybody else. And what have you ever done?"

I put the suitcase in the car and walked back upstairs to get the cage with Charley. He hopped around nervously when I lifted up a corner of the cover. He wasn't used to being moved around at night.

"Where are you going, Jarvis?" Alna said, looking up with red eyes and tear-stained face.

"I don't know, my dear," I said, leaving a small kiss on top of her head. "If the cat turns up, take care of him for me. Corey'll be all right," I said. Fat lot of comfort. I gave Alison a little wave as I departed. "Maybe you'll be back," Alison said wryly.

I had noticed that Corey's car was still parked in front of my old wreck, but I didn't know where she'd gone. She came walking up as I put the bird in the back seat.

"Well," she said, with a little smile and a shrug. "Well," I said, in the same spirit.

"Oh, Jarve, I hope you understand me."

"Of course," I assured her. "It's hard when you can't offer a solid proposition, a bet with reasonable odds if not a sure thing—when all you've got is a guess and a prayer."

"It isn't that I want to run off and screw a bunch of guys or get a job with an advertising agency. It isn't that at all. But . . . Oh, I don't know. I'm just groping in the dark."

"I know," I said. She had company.

"I'm glad you're leaving," she said.

"Well, good luck, darling," I said, putting my arms around her.

Unable to speak, she kissed me and left without another word.

Outside, the night was brilliant with stars. I took a deep breath that lifted heart and lungs. The air smelled of moisture, of things growing in the soil, reaching for their summer. Too bad, I thought, that one had lost so much of the animal he could no longer catch the scent of something fresh in the wind. The smell of earth was reassuring and yet maddening and depressing. What would draw me bounding into that promise? My wings were wet and sticky, and I was still weak and un ready.

I thought of those who were staying behind, visited by rain and snow and all the varying weathers of experience. I could have stayed with them, under the illusion of safety; but it was too late for that. At least I knew where I had gotten my restlessness. I'd held it down for thirty years—now I was a leaf in the wind.

Gladys Swan has published four novels—*Carnival for the Gods* (Vintage Contemporaries Series) and a trilogy set in New Mexico, where she grew up—*A Dark Gamble; Ghost Dance: A Play of Voices* (LSU Press) and *Ancestors*. She has also published seven books of short fiction, including *The Tiger's Eye: New & Selected Stories*. Her poetry and essays have appeared in many literary magazines and anthologies. Though she has spent most of her career as a writer, she has spent much of her time during the last two decades to painting and exploring the creative process.